A beam of [illegible] back and forth.

She nestled [illegible] trembles turned to shakes.

*What if he finds me?*

As the light came closer, a shrieking wail split the night air. A leap of hope held her in place. *Only good guys use sirens, right?* She felt as much as heard running steps pounding the ground close by, then that sound disappeared, replaced by a second siren which battled with the first.

She lifted her head just high enough to watch as several cars screeched to a halt out on the street. People spilled out and approached the house, their dark shapes silhouetted by streetlights. The sirens had cut off, and now rotating lights added an abstract effect that lit their progress.

Her mother had said to stay in her safe place until the police came to find her, but what if they didn't come? How would she know if it was safe to leave her post? She shivered, wishing she'd grabbed her jacket and that weird stuffed panda they'd won at the county fair.

Mom would be okay, she told herself. She'd done exactly what her mother said, and everything would be all right. Thinking about that horrible sound she'd heard, she clamped her eyes shut, repeating that hope in her mind. *It'll be all right, it'll be all right.*

**Praise for Fear the Night:**

*Fear the Night* won the Oklahoma Writers' Federation Inc.'s Romance Novel Category in 2019.

# Fear the Night

by

Dianne McCartney

**Fear the Night**


Contact Information: info@thewildrosepress.com

Cover Art by *Abigail Owen*

The Wild Rose Press, Inc.
PO Box 708
Adams Basin, NY 14410-0708
Visit us at www.thewildrosepress.com

Publishing History
First Edition, 2021
Trade Paperback ISBN 978-1-5092-3583-4
Digital ISBN 978-1-5092-3584-1

Published in the United States of America

## Dedication

This book is dedicated to my late brother, David, who died when I was seventeen.
And, as always, to my beloved husband, Mitch, daughter, Colleen, and new son-in-law, John.

## Acknowledgements

A heartfelt thank you to my wonderful editor, Ally Robertson, and the rest of the hardworking staff at The Wild Rose Press.

**Other Wild Rose Press Titles by Dianne McCartney:**

Just One Night
The Daughter of Death
The Road to Justice

# Prologue

The moment Adrienne Maxwell heard her mother scream their secret word, she ran for the bedroom window as fast as her ten-year-old legs would allow. Yanking it open, she searched the darkness for the escape chute. Her frantic gaze caught sight of the yellow opening anchored to the side of the house, and she jumped in, feet first, as they'd practiced.

She bumped and twirled down from the second floor, landing with a muted thump on the thick, vinyl cushion below. Her legs tingled from the shock, but she pushed herself to her feet, her heart thumping. As she stood, she heard her mother scream again. This time the sound was followed by a strange, banging noise.

Charging across the meadow, she aimed for the shadows of the woods, her path lit only by the full moon. An owl hooted a warning as she entered at a run, then slowed to a scramble so as not to fall. Ignoring the fallen branches that scraped her pajama-clad legs, she headed for the thickest underbrush, panting now, and plunged in, burrowing as deep as she could. Her mother's instructions sounded in her ear as if she stood beside her. *Go deep, as deep as you can, where no one can see you.*

Now that reaction had caught up to her, she began to cry, stuffing her fist in her mouth to try and mute the sound. The stillness of the night meant that when the bad man opened the door, she heard the creak of the hinges and knew that, sooner or later, he would search in her direction.

She listened, hoping that maybe she was wrong, and he had returned to wherever he came from. But it wasn't to be. His feet made a weird, spitting sound as he crossed the gravel driveway.

A beam of light played over the woods, scanning back and forth.

She nestled deeper, and her trembles turned to shakes.

*What if he finds me?*

As the light came closer, a shrieking wail split the night air. A leap of hope held her in place. *Only good guys use sirens, right?* She felt as much as heard running steps pounding the ground close by, then that sound disappeared, replaced by a second siren which battled with the first.

She lifted her head just high enough to watch as several cars screeched to a halt out on the street. People spilled out and approached the house, their dark shapes silhouetted by streetlights. The sirens had cut off, and now rotating lights added an abstract effect that lit their progress.

Her mother had said to stay in her safe place until the police came to find her, but what if they didn't come? How would she know if it was safe to leave her post? She shivered, wishing she'd grabbed her jacket and that weird stuffed panda they'd won at the county fair.

Mom would be okay, she told herself. She'd done exactly what her mother said, and everything would be all right. Thinking about that horrible sound she'd heard, she clamped her eyes shut, repeating that hope in her mind. *It'll be all right, it'll be all right.*

Moments later, the door squeaked open again, and she chanced another peek. Now, the house had lights shining from every window. "Max," someone yelled.

It sounded like Mom's policeman friend, but how could she be sure? All she could see was the dark outline of a tall man. As she watched, someone else joined him, and they crossed the driveway. She heard them talking in muted tones as they came much closer, then stopped. One of them put the flashlight under his chin so that it lit up his face. The move revealed familiar features. "Max, it's me. Please come out, honey. You're safe now."

So relieved she almost peed her pants like a baby, she clawed the brush away from her face. "I'm here, Mr. Jeff." She pulled herself to her feet using an outstretched branch and staggered out from beneath the bushes. When he approached, he bent down so she could see his worried face, then hugged her. She burst into tears.

"Oh, honey, I'm so sorry. You're safe now. Come on with me. We'll get something to warm you up." He clasped her hand as they moved closer to the house where she could see other officers searching the lawn.

"Is my mom okay?"

The two men looked at each other. "Let's go sit in the car for a minute."

She read the tension in their expressions and wailed. "No, no, no. I did just what she said. It's supposed to be okay. She said everything would be okay if I did like she showed me."

Leaning down, Mr. Jeff put his jacket around her shoulders and hugged her.

## Chapter One

*Present day, Twenty-five years later*

Clawing fingers on her neck woke Max, and she battled imaginary demons to sit up, arms flailing. She yanked at her sweat-dampened clothes and realized, with a strangled, inward breath, that the intrusive fingers belonged to her. Her dogs whimpered in the scant morning light.

"It's okay," Max reassured them, her voice trembling. Looking around, she realized she'd fallen asleep in the recliner again. At least there would be no time wasted making the bed. As she stood, every cramped muscle sang out in protest, making her groan. One of her Labradors, Larry, licked her face as she stretched down to move the throw that had slipped off her legs during the night.

"Oh, geez. Brush your teeth," she mumbled. He wagged his tail in response. The other two dogs looked at her expectantly, and she wandered to the back door to let all three of them out for their morning constitutional.

Passing the mirror as she headed to the shower gave her a fright. She didn't look thirty-five this morning. Her dark hair looked like a 1980s back-combing experiment, and she had familiar dark shadows under her eyes.

*Is this an attractive look?*

*Probably not.*

In the shower, she let the warm water beat down on her and started to feel human again, bit by bit. Rubbing shampoo and a cream conditioner into her tangled mane soothed her.

*Who needed sleep?*

Well, she did, but having everything else she ever wanted in life meant maybe she shouldn't get greedy. Toweling off, she peered into her closet to withdraw what she considered her uniform: jeans and a cotton shirt. She coaxed them on over her damp skin.

Sliding on her work boots, she went outside and found the dogs playing down by the barn, their outlines traced against the deep red siding. She moved toward them, searching the field and noticed her horse, Ghost, was nowhere to be found. *Great. Where has he disappeared to now?* She whistled and heard no response. Seeing a flash of gray out of the corner of her eye, she walked closer to the fence line to get a better view.

****

Angus McLaren rubbed his eyes and stared, struggling to comprehend why there appeared to be a horse in his kitchen. He fumbled to reach his glasses from the pocket of his pajama top. When he slid them on, everything sprang into focus. The horse wasn't really in the kitchen. His head protruded through the open window, and his thick, rubbery lips attempted to reach the limp vegetables in the takeout container from the preceding night.

"Good morning," he said, listening to the pre-coffee scratch of his own words. He couldn't think of anything else to say.

The horse tilted his head, taking a break from his quest. Bigger than average, judging by the size of his head, he had glowing dark eyes and grey-white hair with whiskers sprouting all over his muzzle. They stared at each other, then suddenly the horse's ears pricked forward.

Angus heard a voice calling from outside and watched as the horse slowly backed up, tilting his head so it fit through the opening. He couldn't make out the words from outside, just a long "oooo" sound.

Hurrying to the window, he watched as the horse turned and trotted rather elegantly up the slope of his side lawn. When he came to the bordering fence, he leapt over it with uncommon grace.

On the other side of the partition, a lone figure stood in silhouette against the morning sky. Wrapped in a red and black checkered coat, she had long, dark hair that whipped in the autumn wind. The woman held out a hand to the horse as he approached. Reaching up, she rubbed his face, causing the horse to lean into the pressure, an oddly touching gesture.

*So, this is my neighbor*. He struggled to remember the name his friend Ian had told him but drew a blank. As the local police chief, Ian knew everyone from his town. He had called her the 'perfect neighbor,' trying to reassure Angus he was making the right decision, moving to a town Ian referred to, lovingly, as 'Booneyville.'

As Angus watched, the woman and horse disappeared into the barn. Turning back to the kitchen, he looked around him and winced. Even the bright sunshine couldn't make up for the mess on the inside of his new home. *Have I lost my mind?*

At the ripe old age of thirty-nine, he was having a mid-life crisis. That's what this appeared to be, according to his mother, his friends, and the world in general. Having lived in the city all his life, he had come to visit Ian one day and ended up buying a house. Not just any house, but a rundown mess which needed lots of loving care. And he knew nothing about carpentry or plumbing.

But he knew how to hire people to do what he couldn't.

How could he explain to everyone this house, in fact this town, called to him in a way nothing ever had? Ian proved to be the only one who seemed to understand. His friend loved this town and had quite happily shown Angus around when he'd expressed an interest. They saw the real estate sign and stopped when Angus asked.

Ian had even pulled some strings to cajole the agent there within an hour, using the wait to tell him about the house. The inside had been redecorated by someone with a dubious artistic bent. In the seven years the owners lived there, they had butchered the inside with everything from purple carpet to a solar system painted on one wall. The saving grace was that they had left the exterior as is, with big wooden porches and welcoming steps.

He could fix the inside. To be more specific, he could pay someone else to fix it. That would be his first errand today, right after breakfast, locating someone who could accomplish that challenging task.

His stomach grumbled. *Why didn't I think to buy groceries?* He vaguely remembered a restaurant on the main drag Ian had recommended. It would be his first stop, after a shower.

Thirty minutes later, Angus parked next to a sign reading: Boone, Tennessee, Population 26,412. Four hundred and thirteen now, he thought with a grin. He walked down the cracked sidewalk, taking in the beehive of activity around him, and found the sign he recalled—it read, 'Boogie and Bo's.'

The door had a little bell attached at the top, and it jingled to announce his arrival. Decorations inside were all-American red, white, and blue, and the creased vinyl seats looked at least forty years old . Most of them were already occupied. He spied a single table at the back, sensing the gaze of other diners as he made his way there. Ian had warned him about the 'talk' in their town. It seemed now he'd become the focus of some curiosity. He took a seat, trying to remember if he had combed his hair or just ran a hand through. Too late to worry about it now.

A perky little blonde, no more than twenty, sidled up to the table, wiping one hand on her jeans. "Can I get you some coffee?"

He nodded, noting the name, Katie Sue, embroidered on her blouse. "Please. I take it black."

She smiled, showing a row of metal-banded teeth. "No problem. Welcome to Bo's."

"Thank you, Katie Sue. Appreciate it." *What happened to Boogie? Wasn't it Boogie and Bo's?*

She returned quickly with a tall mug of dark coffee which smelled like heaven. A red and white menu covered in plastic got placed down beside the mug.

"You're Mister McLaren, right? You moved into the hippies' place." With a little gasp, she slapped a hand over her mouth. "I'm so sorry—my momma says I can't keep my words straight."

He chuckled. "No harm in speaking the truth."

"It's just, well, they weren't really like us. Nice enough folks, though. Just kinda…artsy, I guess." She grinned. "Nothing wrong with art, right? Some of it's pretty."

"I've got a little too much of the artsy all over the walls."

"Well, then you picked the right neighbor, didn't you?" Smiling, she started to move away.

His brain scrambled to try and catch up. "Neighbor?"

Katie Sue turned back. "Well, it's up to you, but Max fancies up houses all the time, and she's right next door. Real handy-like."

The cook or someone behind the half-wall bellowed, and she scurried away.

Max, he thought, thinking of the figure he saw with his big, hairy visitor. He recalled the name Ian had mentioned with post-coffee clarity—Adrienne Maxwell. He'd have to ask what 'fancying up houses' meant in real terms. She didn't look like a decorator, but what did he know? All he had to go on was one glance. The decorator he'd worked with in Nashville wore high heels, tight skirts, and abundant perfume.

For now, his quick glance at the menu confirmed his wildest hopes for a stack of pancakes with real maple syrup. He could go for a hike later to burn the calories off. The delicious coffee kept him occupied as he waited. When breakfast came, it meant three plates, not one—biscuits, bacon, and grits all part of the picture. He wolfed down every scrap of the pancakes in a flash and took his time with the rest.

Ian entered the restaurant as Angus buttered a biscuit, waving a casual hand to address the chorus of cheerful greetings from other diners. He slid onto the opposite seat from Angus with a practiced air. "Mornin'."

Angus sat back with a groan. "That's the best plate of pancakes I've had in years. I'll have to work out twice a day to avoid gaining weight."

"Welcome to the country. Around here, food is our middle name." His textbook, blond buzz cut and bright blue eyes made him seem like an advertisement for the police department. He was a morning person to boot.

But Angus liked him, despite that.

"You sleep okay?"

Angus nodded. "I had a visitor this morning."

"The ladies after you already?" Ian laughed, slapping his leg. "I warned you, didn't I? Ten chicks for every rooster."

"My visitor was of the large four-legged variety." He recalled the face. "Gray-haired and shaggy."

"Oh…Ghost. You're not scared of horses are you, city boy?"

"What? No, of course not."

Ian chuckled. "That's Ghost. He's harmless. He just likes to visit. Was he waiting on your porch?"

"Stuck his head right in the back window." Angus shook his head. "I could have sworn I shut the damn thing."

"That wouldn't stop him. Why do you think Max calls him Ghost?" Ian stuck an elbow on the table, grinning. "He spends half of his time appearing where he's least expected. Last week, Mrs. Gardner chased him out of her greenhouse with an umbrella."

"The waitress said my neighbor does something with houses?"

Ian leaned over and stole a piece of his bacon, shoving it in his mouth then talking around it. "She renovates and builds houses for a living. I was going to suggest you talk to her, because she does a great job for a fair price. Not all the men around here are happy about that, because she tends to get the best workers. Especially Nate."

He gestured for another cup of coffee, nodding his thanks. "Who's Nate?"

"The best carpenter around here, bar none. He mostly keeps to himself, just him and his little girl, but he and Max are fast friends. He won't work with anyone else."

"Do you have her contact information? I don't want to just wander over."

Ian whipped out his phone. "Want me to call and set it up? I know she's on a job over in Newbury. That'll be where she is right now."

"Great idea. Thanks." He watched Ian punch keys, then eavesdropped, hearing the easy tone between his friend and his neighbor.

Ian finished the call. "Friday night, six, your place, and I conned her into bringing pizza to eat afterward. She drives right past Tony's on the way home—that's why she's picking it up. I told her two large, double meat for us, okay?"

That's one thing Angus loved about the South. Food provided the backdrop for every conversation. "Fair enough. So, tell me about Max."

The waitress slipped a cup of coffee beside Ian, and he nodded his thanks. "She's our age, very happily single, and what the menfolk around here call the 'liberated type.' That means she is independent, enjoys her work, and is feisty enough to tell them all to go to hell when necessary." He laughed. "She's actually a great boss, according to the guys who work for her. Most of them have stayed with her a good, long time."

"So, why isn't she the new Mrs. Ian Cross?"

"Ouch." He rubbed his arm in mock protest for the wound. "She's too much of a handful. You know me. I like the sweet ones who aren't any smarter than me."

Ian had always had lousy taste in women, but that made a subject for another day.

## Chapter Two

The project in Newbury rolled along right on schedule, which made Max itchy, as if she expected some unforeseen delay. She stood at a makeshift table, re-sketching the kitchen island to modify the shape a little, a change the homeowner had requested.

She and Nate rarely sold a house before work wrapped up, but this proved to be an exception. The couple had fallen in love with this property, located just three streets over from where they lived now. On the hunt for a bigger house, they had discovered her project on an evening walk and begged a surprised Max for a tour, buying it as soon as she could cough out a price.

That fortunate turn of events removed the realty fees on this sale. She would happily grab a miracle any day she could. The call from Ian meant that, with a little luck, she could keep her men working non-stop, not always a given in her line of work.

Ian had said her new neighbor's name was Angus. *Kind of an old-fashioned name.* The town scuttlebutt had already leaked a few more details. He was an old college roommate of Ian's, trying out his first home in the country.

When she asked what he did for a living, Ian had just said he was 'an egghead.' *What the hell did that mean?* Somehow the local women had come up with 'single and rich,' and it was game over with all kinds of

Machiavellian schemes falling into place. As usual, she felt like telling them all to, please, get a life which didn't focus on the capture of some unsuspecting man.

Tempted to warn him about the bullseye on his back, Max realized it might be kind of fun to watch all the fuss from a distance.

She'd heard the noise of his arrival early yesterday evening. Her dogs, alerted by the slam of his car door, barked, warning her of his presence. Peeking through her shutters, she saw a tall man with a thick head of dark hair. He'd dragged suitcases and five or six boxes from his SUV, then disappeared inside.

That's all she thought about until this morning, when Ghost had paid him a visit. It had made her giggle, she had to admit, when she thought of the city slicker waking up to a big-ass horse halfway into his kitchen. If he was scared of horses, her charismatic, fifteen-hundred-pound friend would soon cure him.

The house he'd purchased had great bones but needed a total renovation inside. She loved the big, beefy logs with the peaked roof and the sprawling porch, but the artists had butchered the interior. She wondered about the size of his budget. The renovation wouldn't be cheap.

But for now, back to work.

****

The weekdays dragged on as Angus waited for Friday. The extra-long blowup mattress he slept on wasn't living up to its claim of 'maximum comfort for a minimum price.' Even an hour of exercise every morning didn't help much. His joints were paying the penalty. He should have taken Ian up on his offer of a place to stay, but he wanted to get the renovation of the house arranged first.

Every day he watched his neighbor head out in her truck. She honked the horn once, but other than that kept her distance. Her horse was much friendlier, following along the fence as he took his morning walk, keeping pace for a while, then settling down to graze. He hadn't hopped the fence again, but according to Ian, it might be just a matter of time.

Angus enjoyed exploring his house, making notes. He didn't really know what he had planned, but it was fun to imagine what it could look like. It certainly wouldn't be cheap.

When Friday morning finally arrived, he forced himself to drive in and around town to take a long walk, getting to know the layout as well as all the businesses. Some people stopped to introduce themselves, and pretty much everyone at least waved. It ate up a few hours of the day and made him feel more a part of things.

****

Max left the site at 5:30 on Friday evening, allowing plenty of time to pick up the pizza and arrive at Angus's house as promised. She hated being late, the sure sign of poor time management. Being punctual made a good first impression.

She drove with the pizza on the seat of the truck cab, laughing as her dogs sniffed the aroma from the bed in back. They curved their necks toward the open windows. The scent made her stomach grumble in anticipation.

Ian's patrol car sat parked in the driveway when she arrived, along with the black SUV. The two men were waiting on the porch, leaning against the log walls as if they were holding them up. Together, they made an odd couple, the tall and lean newcomer against Ian's short and stocky build.

Climbing out of her truck, she told the dogs to stay in the back. As she walked in the men's direction, she stuck out her hand toward her neighbor as they came down the stairs. "Hi. I'm Adrienne Maxwell. Call me Max." *Gosh, he's tall*. Even though she stood five-foot-ten, he towered over her.

"Hi Max. I'm Angus." He glanced past her. "Nice dogs. Labrador retrievers, right?"

"Yes." *He doesn't seem uneasy*. "Are you okay with dogs? I won't let them out if you aren't, but they're very well behaved."

"Please do."

She gave them the command, "Free," and they jumped out, tails wagging, one yellow and two blacks, to greet him. "Meet Larry, Curly, and Mo."

He laughed as the three dogs sat, in unison, each offering a paw. Leaning down, he shook each one. They dissolved onto the ground, bellies up, begging for a rub. A lifetime dog lover, he obliged. When they tried to follow him into the house, Max pointed to the bottom of the stairs. "Stay." Their disappointed expressions were clearly from long practice, but they settled on their bellies and stretched out.

As they walked in the front door, she tried not to wince. A big mural dominated the generous space of the purple, shag-carpeted living room. *Can artists be color-blind?*

Ian laughed at her expression, and she tapped him on the arm. "Don't laugh. That's not nice."

"It's okay," Angus interjected. "Better to laugh than cry. I don't have great taste, but I'm certain we can do better than this."

"I'm scared about what might be living in that carpet." She wandered past him, staring with incredulity at the swirls of fluorescent paint. Having seen it before didn't improve the experience. "I can help you with this, but what we can achieve depends on your budget and how much you want renovated."

He hesitated, as if unsure of where to begin. "Why don't you tell me what you would do with it, and I'll see what I think."

Max nodded. "Is there anyone else whose needs or taste we have to consider?"

"No."

"Fair enough. Let's walk through each room, then we can sit down and go over everything." She started with the living room, pointing at the one long wall with the mural. "You really should have some built-ins here for a big television and books. Are you a reader?"

"Yes. I have a lot of books."

"He's a total nerd," Ian interjected, and Max ignored him with the ease of long practice.

"I have the best carpenter in town on my team. Nate does very high-quality work. He'd recommend floor-to-ceiling cases with a centered space for the television and electronics. You can tell him what screen size we have to accommodate."

She gestured at Ian, who had already finagled a piece of pizza which he stuffed into his mouth. "Did our pizza thief tell you the realtor indicated this house needs all new electrical and some major plumbing repairs?"

"Yes."

She realized Angus didn't have much to say, and the serious expression in his dark eyes proved hard to read. Leading the way into the kitchen, she sighed. Worse than she remembered, it had a terrible layout and appliances from the seventies, right down to the avocado color. "Do you like to cook?" She opened the oven, shaking her head as it almost hit the refrigerator.

"Yes."

For some reason, that surprised her. "Reheat fast food cook or watch chefs on television for inspiration cook?"

"The latter," he answered with a smile which transformed his watchful expression. Max noticed his eyes were the same rich, golden brown as his hair.

Ian grinned. "Good cook as in I'll come for dinner any time I'm invited and maybe even when I'm not."

*Rather sexist of me to be impressed by that.* "Okay. In that case, this is where you're going to drop a lot of money. Large, top-quality kitchens are high-ticket items. I would suggest tearing everything out and starting from scratch. There's nothing salvageable here. We can begin by opening the kitchen to the living room. That would make it much more spacious."

He nodded.

"You need nice, beefy granite or quartz for your counters, something with attitude, a big mack-daddy gas stove, oversize refrigerator…."

"Pantry."

It sounded funny, hearing a man ask for a pantry, but he knew his stuff. "Yes, good idea. Losing the wall means we can have an extra-large island. I'd open up the back wall, too. The little room on the other side is a waste of space, and it'll add enough room for a big pantry."

When they were through with the kitchen, they reviewed each room along the same lines, moving from turquoise toilets to peeling linoleum. Two smaller bedrooms at the back of the house could be combined to give him a roomy master suite. The other bedrooms mostly needed new flooring and fresh paint.

Afterward, they settled back on the porch on the few ratty old chairs the former owners had left behind and shared the pizza. Max rolled her eyes when she saw Ian steal some from his friend, having already polished off his share.

"It's a lot of work," she said, to make sure Angus understood the scope of the job.

He shifted, clearly trying to get comfortable in the undersized chair. "I knew that when I saw it, but I liked the outside of it and the land so much."

"I think you're the right person to take this on. Not everyone has the vision, but the location is great. It will protect your investment."

He looked at her. "If you're involved in this business, why didn't you purchase it yourself?"

Some might think him too blunt, but she liked the straightforward nature of the question. "The former owners made the decision to sell without much warning. I have three houses in development right now and, unfortunately, cash flow couldn't cover it. It's easy to get overextended in this business."

He nodded. "That makes sense. Do you know how long it will take to have an estimate?"

"I should have it the day after tomorrow around supper time." She would get the bid to him as fast as possible to try and secure the job. "Your kitchen and the electrical will be the biggest ticket items. This house has a great foundation, so I'm not expecting anything there, but we'll do a full inspection to be certain." She set her notes to the side. "Are you going to live here during renovation?"

"Ian said he'd put me up. The blow-up mattress has lost its appeal."

"It'll cost ya." Ian swaggered over, yet another slice of pizza in his hand. "You'll have to cook every night and scrub the bathroom."

Angus raised his eyebrows. "Can anyone look at your bathroom and not run screaming out of the house?"

"Probably not."

"Then I guess I'll have to do it."

Their interplay made for pretty funny schtick, an obvious leftover from their college days. Max stood to leave.

"How much do I owe you for the pizza?" Angus asked as he pulled out a wallet from his back pocket.

"Nada. Consider it a welcome to the neighborhood."

"Thank you."

Ian raised a hand in a victory gesture. "Score. Free pizza. Life is good."

Max glanced back at him as she headed down the steps and loaded the dogs into the back of the truck. "The town bad guys wouldn't be too scared if they knew the real you."

She closed the door on Angus's delighted laugh.

****

Much later, after Ian left, Angus sat on the porch, staring out at the night. The inside of his house might be ugly right now, but peace enveloped him. Once in a while, he could hear a vehicle pass on the nearby road, but mostly he enjoyed the ribbit of the frogs in the nearby pond and the breeze that wandered through the trees. And, in the air, he smelled freedom.

The rest of his life had been spent in city apartments, motels, or on airplanes. And suddenly, unexpectedly, it wasn't enough anymore.

He wanted a home.

And not just a home, but a family.

Time rolled along, a little too fast for his taste. He would never have believed it, but he wanted someone to share his life with and a nice place to lay his head. Always a methodical man, he would start with the house and figure out the rest as he went along.

His cellphone rang, and he glanced at it. His mother. With a sigh, he picked it up. "How's the prettiest girl in Louisville today?"

Her peal of laughter made him smile. "Okay, smooth talker. I'm just dandy. How's my favorite son?"

An old joke of theirs, since he was her one and only. "I'm surprised you're not still calling me your crazy son."

"I'm trying to mind my Ps and Qs." She paused. "Are you happy out there?"

She made it sound like another galaxy. "Actually, I was just thinking I feel more relaxed than I have in years."

"Well, that's all that counts, isn't it? Tell me about the house."

He filled her in on the changes he and Max had discussed.

"Let me get this straight. Your neighbor is a contractor and she's a woman."

He could see where this is going. "If I hire her, yes. And I think I'm going to."

"Is she pretty?"

He thought about the long, shiny hair and her thoughtful expression. And about the curvy body he hadn't missed. "She's girl-next-door pretty."

"That's what you need. You certainly don't need another prima donna."

He couldn't help a grin. The darn woman had a point. "Well, look at the time, I've got to go."

"No, you don't. You're just being a pill."

"You be good, now. I love you."

"Love you, too, Angus."

He adored his mother. He really did. But her first response to his announcement that he planned to move to the country involved a horrified gasp and her immediate assertion he just needed a good woman. While he'd never been averse to the thought, until now he had always been happy on his own, especially since his last very loud breakup with Katia, who threw one of her very expensive high heels right at his head. That had resulted in the long-overdue trip to see Ian and the subsequent revelation about his life.

The fact is, he had experienced great success in his work life and the exact reverse in his personal life. All of a sudden, he knew what he wanted. He just didn't have a clue how to find it.

But he had taken the important first step, and he'd figure out step two down the line. Right now, he planned to have a long, thorough look at the details of every room in his house and get a good night's sleep. Everything always seemed clearer in the morning.

When he rose to go inside, he noticed all of Max's lights still blazed, even at this late hour. Strange, he thought, as he headed for bed.

## Chapter Three

Monday morning, Max drove toward her job site, turning the air blue with a few choice words. This morning, the plumber failed to turn up on time again, and Nate warned her he had discovered the sloppy and unacceptable work the man had done the previous Friday. So, her first job of the day would be to fire someone.

*Damn it.*

It wasn't as if she even liked Todd Priestly, but plumbers weren't that easy to come by, especially on short notice. It would likely mean a few days' delay, precious time lost on a tight schedule. But sloppy had no place in her vocabulary.

She slammed the door of her truck, happy to hear the reassuring whine of a saw. The blare of the radio offered some country star wailing about honky tonks and bad beer.

Nate wandered out to greet her, a glimmer of humor in his eyes. "You look like you're ready to breathe fire." He folded muscled arms across his chest.

"Well, what the hell is his problem?"

He scuffed the toe of his faded work boots in the dirt. "He's lazy. Thinks he's too good to work hard and his pretty face will bail him out of trouble."

She snorted. "I've got your pretty face to keep me company. Why would I need two of you?"

He laughed, passing a hand over his scarred cheek, but stopping her with a hand on her arm. "I think he's got a temper in there, so holler if you need backup."

Max smiled at his concerned expression. For all his huge size, he only used muscle when no alternative presented itself. "I won't, but good to know, as always."

Picking her way around the piles of lumber, she made her way inside, pleased to see they were making steady progress in other areas at least. The few men on site nodded and waved, one or two looking expectant.

She found Todd leaning up against a wall, waving a tool around as he told a story. The others appeared to be ignoring him. "Can you come outside for a moment?"

"Sure, boss," he answered, the derision thick inside the seeming agreement. He wandered behind her, taking his time.

Pausing at the corner of the house, she turned to face him. "You were late again."

"Yup." He yawned. "The ladies keep me up at night, what can I say."

"The work you did on Friday was substandard and unacceptable."

"Says who?" He glanced over at Nate, who stared back.

She moved in front of him to regain his attention. "Says me. I think we've reached the end of the road. You're fired. Please get your tools and leave right now."

He dropped the nonchalant attitude, standing straight for the first time. "Hey, bitch. Who do you think you are?"

"Unfortunately for you, I'm the bitch who owns this company. You'll be paid for Friday, even though we'll be forced to redo your sloppy work. But you will leave this property now and not come back. You won't get any more jobs from me."

He spewed a line of curses which she ignored. One of her crew, Pete, came out of the house carrying the plumber's tools which he and Nate placed in the bed of Todd's truck. Storming to the driver's side, Todd shoved Pete out of the way and jumped in.

After a pause, the engine roared to life. The truck leapt into gear and spun away, gravel spitting. A hand came out of the open window, middle finger raised in an adolescent show of defiance.

She sighed as the men re-joined her. "Thanks, guys."

"Nobody liked him, anyways," Pete offered, a smile transforming his earnest face. A small man, wiry and fit, he moved back into the house.

Nate looked thoughtful. "I'd post a guard here for a few nights. He's the type who'll come back and pull something."

"Good idea." She paused. "Any idea where I can find another plumber?"

"Don't worry. I'll ask around."

At three p.m., Nate left to pick up his little Emma, then the two of them met her at her place to review the bid for Angus's project.

Nate whistled, scanning the long list of materials and labor costs. "Pretty hefty price tag," he said. "Do you think he'll go for it?"

"If it's too high, he can either eliminate part of the renovation or do it over time." She paused to consider.

"If I read him right, he'll do it all now and get it over with. I just hope we'll get the job. He didn't say if he was getting bids from multiple companies. I'm grateful Pete could ballpark the plumbing cost so we could deliver it to Angus tonight."

"Can I go look at the new guy's place?" Nate's six-year-old daughter, Emma, said, pointing out the window at Angus's house. "I seen the outside, but not the inside."

"Saw," Max corrected, before Nate had a chance. She patted her on the head. "We have to wait until he's home, then we'll walk down. Would you like a cookie?"

"Uh-huh," Emma said, a smile lighting up her blue eyes. "Don't I look pretty?" she said, touching her blonde hair which was in two braids trailing from little pink bands.

"I like it. Who's your hairdresser?"

She giggled while Max took note of the blush on Nate's face. "Daddy!"

"You have skills I never suspected."

He gave a mock growl, making his daughter shriek with laughter.

They were interrupted by the sound of a vehicle out front, and Max went to the door, peering at their new arrival. "Looks like Mohammed came to the mountain."

The other two moved to stand beside her. She swung open the door and watched as Angus slid long legs out of his car and stood. "Hi." He stood uncertainly, as if unsure of his welcome, running a hand through his hair.

"Come in. We were just fine-tuning your bid." Max opened the door wider and stepped back into the house as he traversed the driveway.

Relief crossed his face. "Oh, good. I didn't want to be pushy, but I'm anxious to see it."

Nate waved him to a seat at her big, wooden kitchen table and Angus sat, passing a hand over the top of it. "This is beautiful."

"Thanks. Nate made it for me."

He looked surprised. "You made this?"

Nate nodded.

"Would you make something similar for me?"

He hesitated, then nodded again. "This is built with reclaimed barn lumber. I have some similar material at the shop I can let you look at."

"And who is this young lady?" Angus squatted down on his heels to be closer to Emma's height.

"I'm Emma," she said, peeking around Nate. "You're bigger than my daddy. Are you the new guy?"

He laughed, seeming surprised at the label. "I guess I am. My name is Angus."

"That's a funny name."

"Emma!" Nate looked embarrassed.

Angus laughed. "It is kind of a funny name. It's Scottish."

She stepped out from behind her father. "Emma means the prettiest girl in the world. Daddy told me."

"That's neat."

Actually, Emma meant 'universal,' but Max liked Nate's version better. "Emma, why don't you watch your show while we talk to Angus about his house? You can grab a cookie from the jar and take it with you."

"Yes, Max." She turned to open it, extricated the cookie with care, and disappeared into the next room.

Angus stared after her, then smiled at Nate. "What a great kid. You're a lucky man."

"Thanks."

Max handed Angus the stapled bid. "Why don't you look it over and ask me questions if you have any?"

"Great." He remained silent for almost ten minutes, paying rapt attention to every line.

When he sat up straighter and pushed it away, she assumed she could talk without interrupting his train of thought. "If it's too much money up front, you could do part of the work now and the rest at a later date. If you want to do that, we should hit the kitchen first, since you like to cook."

"You're hired."

His words stunned her. "That was fast."

He nodded. "I'm pretty decisive by nature. And I want to do it all. Now I have your concept in my head, I can't wait to see it." Motioning to the table, he continued. "I wanted to see some of Nate's work first, but this tells me all I need to know."

"My house is full of Nate's work, especially the living room."

"Do you mind if I take a peek?"

"Not at all." All three wandered through the open room lined with packed bookshelves, moving around Emma who lay on the brightly patterned carpet with the dogs, very much at home. The dogs' tails thumped a greeting. As he glanced around, he noted the beautifully constructed shelving. Her side tables were works of art with the grain of the wood highlighted.

Angus swept a hand toward the shelves. “This is exactly the kind of thing I’m looking for. You really love working with wood, don’t you? It shows.”

Nate looked surprised. “Yes. Have since I was a kid.”

“Once we get started on the house, can we sit down and talk furniture?”

“Sure.” He paused. “Aren’t you bringing stuff from the city?”

Angus winced. “No. I had some decorator do that. It doesn’t really suit me.”

“Donate it and take the tax write off,” Max suggested.

Angus seemed pleased at the suggestion. “That’s a great idea.” Giving her a studied look, he said, “I don’t want to be pushy, but when can you get started?”

“You’re lucky. We had an unexpected delay on another project, so we can get started by the end of next week. How about next Thursday or Friday? The crew should be wrapping up in Newbury by then, so we can at least get demolition started.”

Now he really smiled, the motion lighting his eyes. “That would be great.”

“You’re still planning to stay with Ian while the work is in process, right? You’re free to check in whenever you want, but you won’t want to sleep here. The dust alone will kill you.”

He nodded. “I’ll tell him to expect me. Do you have an expected time frame for the project?”

“Two to three months. We’ll do our best to keep it at the short end of that estimate, but I can’t guarantee that. A lot depends on the subcontractors’ schedules.”

“I understand. That’s very reasonable.”

After everyone left, the house seemed too quiet. Max headed for the shower, washing the day's dust off with the cool water she preferred. After she climbed into her soft, cotton pajamas, she let the dogs in from the yard, dishing out their food into their stainless-steel bowls in the corner by the window. Nate owned the property behind hers, and she could see him chasing Emma around the yard and hear her delighted shrieks. Night-night, she thought, lowering the blind against the setting sun.

She thought working the job next door would be fun. A total transformation always offered the most excitement, but it also helped to have an easygoing client. Angus might be a little serious and quiet, but she thought he would appreciate the quality of their work.

Picking up her book, she grabbed an apple from the refrigerator and lay down on the couch to read. The dogs settled next to her. As the sky darkened, she rose just long enough to turn on all the lights and the television.

****

The observer watched Max, as he often did, under cover of night. Strange that she closed the drapes at the front and the back of her house, but neglected the windows in the center part, where she spent most of her time. He would scold her about it, but her omission allowed him to enjoy the best view.

He had started the day off in a bad mood, and his co-workers stayed clear. He kept working but cursed and raved to himself about having to move his observation post to the other side of the property where there was less cover. The inconvenient change meant a longer walk back to his truck every night, too. All because some jackass had bought the house next door.

Tonight, he settled down with the sandwich he'd brought with him, ignoring the wet grass that dampened his jeans. He would be eating when she ate and changing position when she did. As they enjoyed their meal, he thought about what he'd discuss if he really sat beside her, sure she would hang on every word. They'd been together for years, enveloped in this unusual relationship that defied easy explanations, destined to be together.

Venturing too close to her house meant unsettling either those nosy dogs or the neighbor, so he'd found a midway vantage point. Closeness was just a state of mind, anyway. A good memory meant he knew every movie she preferred and what kind of food she would normally prepare. In his imagination, he sat and ate his meals with her.

She loved him, and he knew it. He felt it deep in his soul and had from the moment they met all those years ago. Others might see them as being a world apart in every way.

But he knew better.

They shared history, he and Max. Time had proven she needed a strong man to stand beside her. Sooner or later all this feminist nonsense would wear off, and she would be happy to stay at home and care for him. The day was coming, before too long. He could feel it in his bones. She would be so relieved when he took over as the man of the house.

A woman needed guidance and he was more than happy to provide it for her.

## Chapter Four

Angus wondered just how bored everyone would be if they knew exactly what he did for a living. If he called himself an anatomist, everyone stared at him with the blank expression of the confused. If he said he studied the human body, he just received ribald jokes and titters. If he said he specialized in eyes, everyone wanted a free exam.

But he wasn't that kind of doctor.

As a PhD, he had studied eye disease and potential cures for years, but a few years ago he had branched off into an unusual field when asked to help with an FBI case. The murder victim had sustained intentional damage to the eye, and Angus had ascertained exactly how the damage had been inflicted, which led to an arrest. Since then, he had been called in on numerous cases where understanding the injury process proved central to the case. A consultant now, his work life was quite varied. He could manage it all out of a home office, which was best case scenario as far as he was concerned.

When not needed by the FBI or another agency as a consultant, he gave lectures and wrote textbooks. It intrigued him when the agents asked him questions about areas other than his specialty. When he asked the reason for their questions, they responded that he saw things in a more detailed way than they did, and it proved to be helpful. That connection had resulted in an unusual offshoot of his business, assisting in cases where a sense of detachment could be beneficial.

So now, he read a lot about the minds of killers, because it fascinated him. He wasn't sure, though, that a look at one section of his bookcase wouldn't scare a lot of people off. Note to self, he thought. Keep the creepy books in the office, for his eyes only.

For now, he would be working on his laptop on Ian's kitchen table. He made the short drive over to his friend's house, dragging in his one suitcase full of clothes and dropping it in the Spartan spare room. All of his work files landed in a pile on the counter by the refrigerator, and then he poured himself a glass of iced tea and began to write a report. He hadn't budged from his place at the end of the workday when Ian dragged through the front door. An awful odor wafted in with him.

He raised an eyebrow. "No offense, pal, but you smell terrible. What happened?"

Cursing, he replied, "Don't ask. I'm headed to the shower in the hopes that my skin hasn't rotted away."

At the slam of the bathroom door, Angus stood, glancing at his watch. It read a few minutes after seven. Twenty minutes later, Ian reappeared, smelling a lot better.

"I thought you had a date tonight?"

Ian grunted, a frown replacing his usual grin. "I cancelled. Crap of a day from the very start. I'm not in the mood to make nice."

"So you decided to settle for my company instead? What, are you nuts? A sexy redhead versus me?" He tried not to smile, but it took effort. Judging by the expression on Ian's face, it might not be the night to tease him.

"You cook better. And you don't count the beer I drink and nag me about how many calories are involved."

"True." He looked in the refrigerator. "Loaded burgers and homemade fries, okay?"

"I might have to marry you."

"You're not my type." He opened a beer with a snap and handed it to Ian. Washing his hands, he pulled implements out of the cupboard and began preparing dinner. "So, what happened to put you in this charming mood?"

Ian voiced a litany of frustrations, rather mundane ones. "And then, just when I thought I'd had enough, I break up a domestic and the idiot drunk of a husband pukes all over my pants."

Angus burst out laughing, strangling it when he suffered Ian's glare. "I thought you were the bigwig around here. Why didn't you let a deputy deal with it?"

"Never enough of them to go around," he grumbled. "To hell with it. I just need some food and a few beers." He rubbed his face. "How about you? Anything exciting going on?"

"Nothing compared to your day," he commented. "I had to break it to a fellow scientist that he butchered all of his samples and needs to restart his experiment over again from the beginning. I am not his favorite mentor anymore, to say the least."

"Egghead issues."

"Exactly."

Preparing dinner took about thirty minutes, and Angus just let Ian vent about his frustrations. He preferred to listen, anyway. When dinner was ready, they turned on the television and headed for the couch. Ian spent most of his time watching sports, and Angus pretended to like it, although he would have preferred some variety. *Don't look a gift host in the mouth.*

"Oh, crap. I meant to tell you Max can start on demolition tomorrow. She asked if you could bring the keys by the house before eight a.m."

A jolt of energy filled him at the news. "Where did you see her?"

"At lunch. I guess she and Nate had an appointment with a potential client. They spend half their life at Bo's." He shoved a fry in his mouth and talked around it. "If you don't want to be there that early, she said to call, and she'll drop by to pick them up."

His burger tasted great if he did say so himself, and he took a minute to finish chewing. "No. You know me. I'll be ready to go by then."

"I figured."

The next morning, he arrived by seven-thirty to open the house for the crew and hand the keys over to Max. She arrived five minutes later, walking down the hill, the dogs trailing behind. "This is the best commute I've had in years," she said with a smile. "Are you getting used to small town life?"

"It's pretty quiet compared to the city."

"And is that a good thing for you, or do you miss all the racket?"

He laughed. "I don't miss it at all, which is a little surprising, considering I've lived there all my life." Looking around, he asked, "Is Nate taking his little Emma to school?"

She nodded. “It’s their favorite time together.”

“Is there a Mrs. Nate?”

An expression of annoyance flitted over her face. “The ex-Mrs. Nate, Sherisse, took off into the unknown before Emma turned one, looking for more excitement than she could find here.”

“Sorry. Awkward question.”

“No, not at all. It’s no secret. In fact, Emma’s much better off without her.”

He shrugged. “Nate appears to be an excellent father, and you are an appropriate female model for her to emulate.”

*Egghead alert*. Hard not to like him, though. She looked up as two loaded pickup trucks turned into the drive. “Here come my guys.” As a couple of men exited the first truck, she walked over to the truck bed and pulled out a construction helmet, handing it to him. “You can hang around as long as you like, but you need to stay out of the way and wear this at all times. No exceptions. That way, no one gets hurt.”

“That’s more than fair.”

She introduced him to the four men, whose names he would struggle to remember. They seemed friendly enough. Within minutes, they were tearing into the multi-colored walls with impressive vigor. After the first hour of swinging blows and piled debris, out came the turquoise toilet and the avocado stove, into the newly delivered dumpster he hadn’t even noticed sitting by the side of the house. Now and then, he would hear a shouted question and Max’s reply.

When he peeked in two hours later, the whole wall between the living room and the kitchen had disappeared, with only dangling wires and a few bent nails as testament to its existence. He could understand her fascination with this work. To be able to see a huge change in such a short time was remarkable.

Angus stayed until lunch, interspersing his study of the house with walking his property, moving from the open lawn to the ring of trees and field around the outside. Max's dogs followed him; he hoped she didn't mind. They took turns peeing on every available tree. The alternative sprinkler system amused him. As he finished the circuit and approached the front door, he noticed the trucks had disappeared. "Everyone gone to eat lunch?"

Max nodded, leaning a push broom against the far wall. "Your property's so close to town, they probably headed to Bo's."

"Whatever happened to Boogie?" he asked. "The name is Boogie and Bo's, right?"

"Boogie ran off with the UPS man two years ago. Bo's too cheap to buy another sign." She laughed. "I wouldn't bring it up if I were you."

"I won't. Your dogs kept me company on my walk. I hope you don't mind."

She shook her head. "They never wander farther than this place or Nate's," she answered. "If they annoy you, ever, just tell them to go home. They will."

"I love dogs, actually, so they won't bother me."

She shrugged. "What's not to love, right? Is getting a dog on the long list in your head?"

"How do you know I have a list?" Her understanding his inclination to do so intrigued him.

Laughing, she leaned down to pat Mo. "It's in your blood, right? Buy a house, check. Renovate it, check. You've got efficiency written all over you."

An inadvertent flush warmed his cheeks. “Guilty as charged.”

“There’s nothing wrong with that,” she replied. “You probably get a lot more accomplished than most do.”

“True.” He smiled. “Speaking of such things, I’d better go and do some work to help pay for the items on my always expanding list.”

“What is your actual occupation if you don’t mind me asking? Ian just said egghead, which doesn’t tell me a lot.”

Angus laughed. “He’s not far off. I study the human eye.”

“As in PhD, university professor type thing?”

“Pretty much. I’m a consultant now and usually work from home with an occasional trip here or there.”

She laughed. “Well, I’d better take my rapidly diminishing I.Q. back to my place and grab some lunch. Demo should be done around four if you want to take a look later.”

****

“So, what did Angus think of the house?” Nate asked as they sat around her kitchen table after work.

Max shrugged. “He seemed pretty excited. Hung around all morning, walking the land and checking in on the progress.” She drank a mouthful of soda. “I guess he’s an authority on eyeballs.”

“You’re joking.”

“Nope. In fact, I looked him up online while I ate lunch and, apparently, he’s a big deal. He’s written a bunch of textbooks and even worked with the FBI and other law enforcement.”

“What in hell would an eyeball guy do with the FBI?”

She shivered. “From the sound of one of those articles, I don’t think we want to know. Icky eyeball crime, I guess.”

Nate laughed. “Seems like a nice enough guy, though.” He stood up, stretching. “You mind if I let Emma have a ride on Ghost before we head home? She’s been nattering about it since I picked her up from school.”

“Sure.” She stood up to join him and heard Emma’s shriek when she found out where they were headed. They stopped by the barn to grab her tiny hard hat and a bridle. She bounced in place as they waited by the gate. Max whistled for Ghost.

On the far side of the pasture, he jumped into a gallop for a few strides before slowing to a trot, then a walk as he approached. Coming to a halt in front of them, he nuzzled for the expected treat, getting a carrot from Emma. “His lips tickle,” she giggled. Once her horse finished chewing, Max put on the bridle, slipping it over his ears to buckle the throatlatch, then Nate lifted Emma to his back. Ghost turned to sniff her leg, and Max could have sworn he grinned.

Knotting the reins off to lay on his neck, Max got ready to lead as Emma grabbed the last tuft of mane to hang on to for safety. They walked together along the fence line, Max at her horse’s head. Nate kept pace alongside with a steadying hand on her thigh, just in case. Ghost, used to this routine by now, took slow, easy steps, his ears flipping back to hear Emma’s chatter.

They continued for three big loops in each direction and then called it quits, immune to the expected moans from Emma. “It’s time for his dinner,” Max explained, putting an end to the drama.

After they brushed Ghost off, Nate and Emma headed off for a meal and bed. Dishing out a scoop of sweet feed from the barrel in the barn, Max left Ghost munching from his bucket beside the water trough.

Just before midnight, she went to grab a glass of milk from the refrigerator and noticed a light by her neighbor’s front porch. She peeked through the blinds to take a closer look. With a start, she recognized Angus’s tall form, silhouetted by the light from a hung lantern. He appeared to be simply sitting, staring out at the darkness. She wondered if he was a night owl, too.

****

The observer entered the local bar and sat, shoulder to shoulder, with a few other people from work. Pretending to listen, he heard nothing of their rambling conversation. His attention focused instead on that moron, Todd Priestly, mouthing off, as always. Now and then, Max’s name would drift his way, accompanied by some obscene gesture or filthy language. Each time, howls of laughter from his idiot pals greeted his pathetic antics.

It disgusted him.

A degenerate like that had no business being in the same universe as his beloved.

Blistering anger surged through his body as he gulped down another frothy mouthful of ale, pretending to smile as one of the guys told a story. His mind raced. The time had come to teach Todd a lesson, and the burgeoning idea of how to do it thrilled him. Getting rid of this bottled-up feeling of frustration would be an added benefit.

He finished the last swallow of his beer and called goodnight to the others, smiling at their waitress as he always did on his way out.

Be predictable. Being average—the one thing at which he excelled.

When Todd stumbled out of the bar almost an hour later, he waited in the dark, shadowed edges of the generous parking lot. He'd carefully planned his every move during the wait. Todd would have to pass by this spot to reach his pickup. The baseball bat kept in his truck felt heavy and reliable in his hand, more than enough to get the job done.

Todd cursed and staggered by, keys dangling from one finger. Max's protector followed. Two surging steps positioned him so he could hit a glancing blow off the other man's head. It made a satisfying thud. His target crumpled to the ground, the only sound beside the strike a harsh exhale of air. As Todd twitched on the ground, facedown, the watcher followed it up with three hits, then four, against his body, counting them in his mind. Pausing, out of breath from the effort, he saw some blood spatter on the pavement, a testament to his skill.

Suddenly, he heard muffled voices coming from the open front door of the bar along with the distant blare of music. He disappeared into the bushes, hopping over the neighboring fence and running to his truck parked on the far side of the warehouse next door.

Changing into his spare T-shirt on a darkened side street in case he'd been seen, he dropped the bat into a convenient sewer drain. All of the house lights were out at this time of night, so he wouldn't be noticed.

He forced himself to cruise below the posted speed limit to his neighborhood convenience store, waiting for his adrenaline to ebb. Showing up with a smile and a few words to the familiar clerk, he bought a handful of candy bars. Alibi covered, just in case, he thought with a smile.

*No need to worry. God protects avenging angels.*

## Chapter Five

Max hadn't been at work very long the next day when she heard a car approach. Looking out the window, she recognized Ian in his patrol car. He got out, glancing around and saying hello to one of the guys. She and Nate met him on the front steps, knowing a visit during work hours didn't bode well. Her concerns burst out of her. "It's not Angus, is it?"

His forehead wrinkled as he shook his head. "No. Why?"

"Nobody's seen him today. When you pulled up, I just thought—"

"No worries. He had some errands in the city," he replied. "No, I'm afraid I'm here about Todd Priestly."

*Yup, it's been that kind of week.* She sighed. "What's he up to now?"

"Actually, he's up to a fortune in hospital bills."

Feeling blindsided, she stuttered, "W-what?"

"Somebody laid a serious whoopin' on the boy late last night in the parking lot of Henry's place."

"How bad?" Nate asked.

He grimaced. "Bad enough that even I could feel sorry for him. He's got a fractured skull, a broken arm, and a punctured lung caused by a broken rib."

"Did he say who did it?"

Ian shook his head. "He's only been conscious a while. Said he never saw his attacker. Bastard hit him from behind." He sighed. "Reason I came to tell you is that apparently he was bad mouthin' you at the bar right before it happened. Did you see him yesterday?"

"No. But I heard he's been trying to stir up trouble since I fired him."

"Dumbass just won't learn his lesson." Gesturing to the notebook he held in his hand, he said, "I have to get your whereabouts for last night, just to cover the bases. I gather you were at home?"

"Yes."

Nate nodded. "Me, too. At home, doing schoolwork with Em."

"Sorry, you guys. I've gotta do a proper follow up to keep everybody happy."

"Don't worry about it, Ian. Have you got any suspects?"

He shook his head. "Probably finally pissed off the wrong guy. We'll look into it, but I don't have a lot of hope. We didn't find a weapon. The doctor said it looked like a baseball bat or something like it. Todd's not exactly a town favorite."

"That's an understatement. Still, I'm not sure anyone deserves to be beaten like that."

"True. Well, I better head back." He made his exit, leaving them to speculate.

"You don't see that kind of vicious crime around here too often," Max said, re-entering the house.

Nate followed her. "Probably a jealous boyfriend or husband who finally had enough of his crap. And even if someone saw something, they likely won't share much information. They'd just figure he probably deserved what he got."

"Not our business, anyway, thank goodness. Let's get back to work."

****

Angus had planned to organize chapters for the new textbook he was writing, but, instead, he hung out on the porch, staring at the night sky. There had been something almost poetic about the way Nate's little girl rode Ghost down the pasture the previous night, silhouetted by the setting sun. It touched him, especially the squeals of glee which had caught his attention in the first place. Not an artistic person, he could still envision it as a painting, something a parent would treasure forever.

He'd never been particularly sentimental, but lately he found himself searching for more: more meaning, more substance, more potential. You couldn't find that in a textbook. He knew he tended to be too analytical at times, but trying to change didn't come easy.

Standing, he stretched and finished off the last gulp of soda. Tomorrow, he would go and buy himself a new chair for this porch, so he didn't have a crick in his neck every time he sat here.

Rambling around the house the next morning, Ian told him about the monthly farmer's market in one of the local parks. "And today's the day. First Saturday of each month." He dug into his scrambled eggs with gusto.

Since Ian seemed unduly pleased with the prospect, Angus asked, "And you're going? Doesn't seem like your kind of thing."

"It's good for me to be seen promoting local businesses." He grinned. "And women outnumber men by about ten to one."

Since Ian's attitude toward women hadn't changed since college, Angus shouldn't be surprised. Other than his disastrous, youthful marriage, he had always believed juggling three women was better than settling for one. Angus thought it sounded exhausting. Figuring out one woman at a time had proven to be enough of a challenge for him.

The clear, sunny morning beckoned. He decided to join Ian, intrigued by the idea. By mid-morning, they strolled the aisles, surrounded by a surprisingly large crowd. Teenagers sauntered by, giggling and pointing at the nudes displayed by a local artist, while younger children were shepherded by watchful parents. "Folks come from all of the surrounding towns, too," Ian explained. "We have the lowest booth fees in the area which keeps vendors coming back."

The array of goods available boggled Angus. Homemade breads with tantalizing smells shared space with pottery makers and quilters hawking their wares. Every manner of fresh vegetable could be found, the local farmers happy to cut out the middleman and sell directly to their customers.

A small bluegrass band wailed in the far corner, a rumpled hat flipped over on the grass in front of them to encourage tips. "Walk the whole thing once to see what you might want to buy, and then we'll go through again and pick it up," Ian suggested. "That way, you know you're getting what you want, and you don't have to lug it around."

Angus thought he might want one of everything. The scent of the bread proved irresistible, and he purchased two loaves. He even discovered some rhubarb jam, his favorite from childhood. He bought two jars, and it gave him a guilty conscience. "I've gained three pounds since I arrived. At this rate, I'll look like Santa Claus by Christmas."

"Unlike some of us, you have six-foot-four to spread it over," his friend replied, looking up. "You'd better suck the extra three pounds in, pal, because here come the ladies." Sure enough, three women made a beeline for them, beaming smiles in place. Ian made the introductions, flirting with all three. After a chat, they eventually moved on. "Where's your game? Your parts haven't atrophied, have they?"

"What?" Angus asked, genuinely confused.

Ian rolled his eyes. "Did you really just ask those fine-lookin' ladies what they thought about the weather?"

"It seemed appropriate, given that I don't really know them." At Ian's sigh, he felt the need to defend himself. "I got a little distracted by the manic way the brunette kept flipping her hair."

Ian laughed, slapping his hand on his leg. "That's Mary's trademark 'Come and get it' gesture. It went right over your head, didn't it?"

Angus shrugged. "They weren't really my type."

"All three?" Ian scorned. "Maybe you're just out of practice."

"I'm picky and old enough to realize that's a good thing." He turned and continued down the aisle, surprised to see Nate standing in front of a tented stall, his little girl at his heels. On approach, he saw Max standing under the bright blue canopy by a big wooden chair. "Good morning."

"Hi, Agnus." Emma made it sound like Agnes, which made him smile.

"Good morning, Emma. Are you buying yourself a chair?"

She giggled, shaking her head so hard her bangs fell over her eyes. "No, silly. My daddy makes them. We put the money in a big jar to go fun places."

"That's a great idea." He ran a hand over the back of the sturdy Adirondack chair. "Can I try it?"

Emma nodded and took his hand to lead him while the others observed, clearly amused, as he lowered himself into the chair. It fit as if it had been custom made for him. Prattling on, she sat on the arm. "Are you gonna buy it? If you buy it, we can go get some cookies."

"Emma, give the poor man a chance to relax," Nate pleaded.

Angus laughed. "Actually, it's perfect. I'm tired of squeezing into the leftover on my porch. Do you mind dropping it off at my house on the way home?"

"No problem," Nate answered. "It's my last one anyway. You can just pay me then."

"Great. Thanks."

Max stood, stretching. "So, what do you think of our little market?"

"It's a lot larger than expected, actually. I feel better about having a house to fill when I come here."

Ian poked him in the ribs. "I told him it's the best pick up joint around, but he doesn't seem to appreciate that." He looked at Nate and Max. "Neither do these two."

Nate and Max looked at each other and shrugged. "We're too old," they said, in unison.

"Jinx," Emma said. "Daddy, can we walk around and buy stuff with Agnus?"

"Sure. Why don't we put his chair in the truck first?"

They ended up in a motley group, roving all the delights of the fair. Everyone seemed to know everyone, and the folks they talked to along the way were very welcoming to Angus. One old lady called him 'a tall drink of water,' and he wasn't quite sure how to respond.

He bought a package of the woman's homemade cookies without quite knowing how it happened. "Well, look at you, charming all of the ladies," Max joked as they walked away. He turned to respond, only to find a well-dressed man edging past him to almost stand on Max's toes.

"Well, hello, beautiful," the man crooned, looking Max up and down with a predatory leer. "You're a sight for sore eyes."

"Hello, Alan," she answered, the pinched lines of her face speaking volumes as she took a step back.

The man didn't seem to be able to read her body language. He smoothed manicured fingers over his slick, blond hair as he grabbed one of her hands, preventing her continuing retreat. "I was just about to try and find some decent food in this godforsaken hole. Why don't you join me?"

"Because she already has plans with me," Angus interjected. "I don't believe we've met. I'm Angus McLaren." He moved a step closer to peer down at the other man, offering his hand.

The other man shook it, crunching his fingers in a rather adolescent bid for supremacy. He gave Angus an assessing glance from glacier eyes. "Alan Patterson. I own Patterson Legal Services here in town." He smirked, straightening his designer tie as he glanced at Angus's jeans and shirt. "What is it you do, Mr. McLaren? Are you one of our local farmers?"

"I'm a scientist."

That caught him a little off balance, judging by the slip in his sneer. "So, what, you teach science at the high school?"

Angus noticed a budding grin at the corners of Max's mouth. "No, I write textbooks, mostly." He took Max's arm. "It's very nice to meet you, but I'm afraid we have to rejoin our group." He spied Nate and sped up to catch the others, Max beside him.

"Thanks," she said, struggling to keep pace.

He slowed and smiled. "It was my very great pleasure."

"I could see you were having fun," she accused, laughing. "But no one else could fault you. You were very…"

"Appropriate," he said. "I'm always appropriate." He enjoyed the carefree sound of her responsive laugh.

"Oh, yes," she answered. "Very appropriate."

When they caught up with the others, Nate asked, "I saw the asshole bothering you again."

She patted his arm. "Angus managed to put him in his place. No worries."

"He's been a problem before?"

Nate nodded. "He asked her out, and she had the nerve to say no, repeatedly."

*Apparently, this Patterson guy needs a lesson on what 'no' means.* "Perhaps he needs clarification. Maybe 'not in this lifetime' might work." A feeble attempt at humor, but it made her smile.

"He's harmless," Max said, waving a hand. "And besides, it makes me laugh a bit. I mean, his father owns the firm, not him. His father has bought everything for him, including, I'm sure, all those over-priced duds he likes to wear."

Angus frowned. "Still living on daddy's dime? How old is he?"

"Way too old to be taking handouts from his parents," she replied. "Now, come on. I'm going to buy you a corndog to reward your chivalry."

Soon after, they went off in separate directions with Nate following him to the house to drop off his new chair.

Early that evening, Angus sat on his porch, trying it out. He would have to remember to ask Nate to make a matching one so he would have one available for company. Sipping on the beer he'd brought with him, he found himself wishing the house had already been renovated. As much as he liked Ian, the walls were closing in after two weeks, and he probably had at least another six weeks to go.

Like tonight, for example. Ian planned to bring a girl home with him, which was all well and good, but Angus didn't want a replay of college days. Having a closeup view of his friend's sex life didn't appeal, especially when it came to squeaky bedsprings and breathless moans.

Maybe he was jealous. He sighed. Hell, there was no maybe about it.

This comfortable chair suited him, but he didn't think the neighbors would appreciate it if he started spending his nights sleeping in it. Deep in thought, he didn't notice the approaching dogs until they were almost at his feet. The trio suddenly appeared through the early dusk, panting, in a semi-circle around his chair. “Hi, guys.”

They answered with wagging tails. Max followed behind them, a plate in her hand. “We didn’t wake you, did we?”

“No. Just thinking.”

“Big, brainy thoughts, when you’d rather be left alone?”

Smiling, he shook his head and started to stand. “Here, take my seat.”

She plunked down a small plate of cookies on the arm of his chair and pulled up the old ratty one. “This is fine.” Settling in, she added, “You didn’t buy these cookies, and you missed out.”

“I only got the first one out of the package I bought. Ian ate the rest.”

“Ian eats every damn thing.” She shook her head. “I don’t know why he doesn’t weigh five hundred pounds. You didn’t miss much, though. Try these ones to compare, and you’ll see what I mean.” She offered him the full plate, and he chose one.

The burst of chocolate tasted so rich it startled him, and the coconut made them chewy. He embarrassed himself by groaning, then apologized. “These are amazing.”

“I knew you’d like them. I’d worry about your lack of taste if you didn’t.” She broke a piece off one and popped it in her mouth, chewing. “Nate and I split a big package of them once a month. They’re the only ones we’ve found worth the calories.”

“You and Nate—you’re just friends, right?”

She nodded, still chewing.

"For how long?"

Swallowing, Max smiled. "Since we were kids. We grew up two towns over, in Macon." She cocked her head. "Why are you sitting out here? It'll be dark soon."

"I find it quite peaceful."

"And…"

He chuckled. "And Ian has a friend over to visit."

"Oh, my goodness." She rolled her eyes. "That's awkward. You'd think he might rein in those hormones for a few weeks."

"I don't mind. Besides, I've been thinking about pitching a tent, as it were."

"Really?" She cocked her head, grinning. "No offense, but you don't seem like the type to sleep on hard ground and cook around a campfire."

"Well, maybe nothing that extreme. My bones don't appreciate solid ground as a mattress. But perhaps a trailer might fit the bill. I guess motor home would be the more appropriate term." He envisioned it. "I could park it somewhere close to the back of the house. That way, I'd have some privacy and be able to enjoy the property while you're working."

Max grinned. "Look at you. Given enough time, we'll turn you into a country boy." She paused. "You'll need a generator to run the appliances, but, other than that, I don't see why you couldn't." Standing, she stretched. "Well, time to head home."

"Stay for a while and help me polish off the cookies."

She gestured at the setting sun. "No, it's getting dark."

"I'll protect you," he said, in jest. He noted her abrupt withdrawal as she frowned and stepped away. "I was joking, of course. I didn't mean to offend."

"Oh, I know," she answered with a forced smile. "Work in the morning, you know. Bright and early." With a parting wave, she whistled at the dogs and headed back to her house with them trotting beside her.

## Chapter Six

Angus stayed in place, thinking about Max's retreat as the sun slid below the horizon. She had closed herself into her house, and he noticed all her lights flicking on, one by one. Was he over-thinking her behavior? No, he didn't think his analytical mind had come to the wrong conclusion this time.

Max was scared of the dark. One of his nerdier interests as a college student had been phobias. Nyctophobia was the clinical name. Hard to believe this strong, intelligent woman suffered from such a thing, but he knew phobias didn't follow the natural rules of reason. And this fear in particular could be tied to a traumatic event she associated with darkness. Maybe this explained why he never saw her out at night. *Is that why Nate lives so close by?*

Lots of questions and no answers, he thought with a sigh. Standing, he pushed his chair back against the house, checked the locks, and headed for his vehicle. He would use the foam earplugs he'd purchased at the pharmacy and try to get some sleep. Tomorrow, he would investigate the various options for a trailer.

In the morning, he woke to find a text from Max, sent at three a.m. It provided the name of a man to call in case he decided on a motorhome. He mentioned his idea to Ian as they ate breakfast. "What's up, old man? My place isn't good enough for you all of a sudden?"

Angus laughed, knowing his friend wouldn't take offense. "I want to enjoy the property, and I'll sleep a little better out there, I think."

"Ha ha," Ian responded. "I guess things got a little noisy last night, didn't they?" He puffed out his chest. "Haven't lost my touch."

"Apparently not. She headed out rather early, didn't she?"

Ian nodded. "She works at the hospital cafeteria and had the morning shift."

Shortly after nine, Angus called and made an appointment with the rental manager Max had recommended. Ian dropped him off at the location close to the main highway. By noon, he had signed the rental on the home on wheels he liked the best and taken a lesson on how to drive the cumbersome vehicle to his property.

Relieved to maneuver it into the driveway, Angus searched Nate out to help him locate the best level place to park. They decided to put it in back of the house, close to Max's fence, for both security and privacy. "That way, if your generator ever quits, you can patch an extension cord into Max's place."

They stood back to inspect the trailer, stem to stern, amused when Ghost came to the fence to check it out. He gave it a loud snort and whinnied, shaking his head.

"I guess that's his stamp of approval," Angus said, laughing.

Nate nodded. "You better hope he doesn't find a way to break in and join you in there. Mind if I take a look?"

"Help yourself."

Opening the door, he glanced inside, scanning from one end to the other. "The bed big enough for you?"

"It is if I sleep diagonally," he answered. "I'm used to that sort of accommodation."

"With Emma's curiosity and Ghost, you might wish you had stayed at Ian's."

Angus smiled. "I like kids and animals, so I think we're good." He thought he read the look of concern on Nate's face correctly. "I won't, of course, invite her inside without your presence."

Nate blushed, the look at odds with the angry scar on his face. "You probably think I'm being over-protective."

Angus shook his head, thinking of some of the scary headlines he'd seen involving children. "Not at all. She's a treasure, and you don't know me at all. I can't think of anything more important than a father looking out for his child."

"Thanks for understanding." He started to move off.

"Nate?"

The other man turned back.

"Is Max frightened of the dark?"

He looked surprised, then clearly struggled for a tactful answer.

"Never mind," Angus said. "I shouldn't have asked. Sorry. I'm a curious person by nature."

Nate sighed. "She has some pretty tragic stuff from her childhood she doesn't like to talk about. It's had an effect, I guess you could say." He scratched his head. "Are the lights going to bother you when you're sleeping this close?"

"I'm a night owl, anyway, so no problem. I was just being nosy."

"I guess, in your business, curiosity is a necessity."

That's rather interesting, Angus thought, that Nate understood. "Yes, it's a benefit, for sure."

With a nod, the other man left, heading to his home.

Mid-afternoon, Max called him over to the house to show him the rotting floorboards in one bathroom they'd been surprised by and would have to replace. "They obviously had a leak at some point and didn't do a proper repair. Luckily, everywhere else, they appear to be fine." Next, she took him to the kitchen area and offered him three different options for ceramic tile flooring and granite countertops. He had no problem selecting his favorites right away.

"Oh, thank goodness. I was worried you'd be like a lot of men and pick gray and beige everything." She rubbed her hands together.

"I let a decorator choose the décor in my last apartment, and everything ended up some version of gray. I hated it and found it depressing. I wanted a completely different look for this place." He considered her positive reaction to his selections. "Are those the choices you would have made for yourself?"

"Yes. I like warm colors with bright accents. I think it's a more cheerful combination."

"I agree." He looked around at the most recent changes. "We seem to be making excellent progress."

"Still ahead of schedule, and we'll try to stay there." She set the samples back on the workbench. "Are you satisfied with the motor home? I guess if the walls close in, you can always sleep under the stars. Ghost would keep you company."

"I think it will work out perfectly," he answered. "The manufacturers make them with all the bells and whistles now. I was quite impressed." He sighed. "I have to be away on a business trip most of next week. Perhaps you can keep an eye on it for me since you're on site anyway."

"Be glad to." She smiled. "You don't sound too enthusiastic. Who do you need to impress this time?"

"It's another conference, so I'll be just one egghead amongst a carton of others."

****

While work obligations occupied Angus the next week, Max filled the wee hours of the night with some research. His name popped up as the keynote speaker at the conference, not just another attendee as he'd implied. She liked his humble nature, but his stature in his field proved a little intimidating, nonetheless. Social media pictures showed a standing-room-only audience for his lecture. Pictures of the dinner and reception showed a woman clinging to his arm, her abundant cleavage heaving.

*Okay, that's my imagination.* Still, she thought a predatory hunger lurked in that gaze. He didn't appear to reciprocate the attention, though. In the closeup, Angus's eyes looked a little strained. The social expectations of his job might not be his favorite thing. She could certainly sympathize.

Out of curiosity, she located a few of his papers that were published in scientific journals. Hardly a dummy, she gave up halfway through the first page. It read like another language.

On Saturday afternoon, noticing Angus had returned, she wandered down the hill to chat. The pleasant weather offered warm sun with no wind. He sat outside under the trailer canopy, staring at his computer with Ghost hanging his head over the nearby fence. When she spied the open laptop, she turned around to go back, not wanting to interrupt his work.

"Where are you going?" he called.

She turned back to face him as he pulled off his reading glasses. "I didn't realize you were working. I don't want to interrupt."

He indicated the chair next to him. "You're not interrupting. Have a seat." When she did, he continued. "I was just writing the requisite thank you emails for the conference."

"If you were the keynote speaker, surely they should be thanking you."

He cocked his head. "Been doing some research, have we?"

Max realized, too late, she'd given herself away. "Guilty as charged. I could tell you were being modest, and it made me curious."

"I don't think of it as being modest. I just think there are a lot of other more interesting things to talk about."

"Such as…"

"Such as why you chose to go into the construction business. I would assume that a female boss is quite rare in your field."

"Yes." She leaned back, crossing her legs. "I'm not sure it would be too interesting to anyone else," she replied. "Nate and I always had this dream about creating a happy home. We would build forts out of tree branches and pretend they were mansions."

"Creating a better future for yourselves."

"Exactly." She found it a little creepy he understood her so well.

"I can't imagine a healthier reaction to adversity. So, why didn't your scenario involve you two as a couple?"

Max stared at him, aghast. "Yuck. It'd be like dating my brother."

He chuckled. "Haven't you ever wondered why?"

She had, actually. "I guess the dynamic was different right from the start."

"No chemistry?"

Grinning, she said, "Well, not that kind of chemistry, anyway."

"I like him. He seems like an honorable man."

"Nate's the best. And he's a great father, too." She tucked one foot underneath her. "Which is kind of a miracle, considering he grew up with a loser for a father and a passive mother who couldn't protect him."

Angus met her gaze. "Is the scar on his face a product of his family history?"

*He sure asks a lot of questions*. "What, have you got some kind of crystal ball or something?" She shoved her hair back out of her eyes. "That was very discreetly worded, by the way. I guess being observant is part of your job."

"It doesn't hurt. I just noticed the scar looked old, not recent."

Max nodded. "It's from a beer bottle, lovingly applied by his drunken ass of a father when he was seventeen." She noted his angry expression and could tell her response jarred him. "That bothers you."

"I dislike cruelty, whether it's applied to animals or people." He paused. "Nate is pretty big. The old man's lucky he didn't rip him to shreds."

She shrugged. "It's not in him. Despite his size, he's the most gentle person I know." Tit for tat, she figured. "How about your parents?"

"My dad was a workaholic who died seven years ago. My mom is a pistol. You'd adore her. Everyone does." He smiled and genuine warmth reached his eyes. "Carolina Angelique McLaren. Lina for short. She thinks I'm currently losing my mind. I'm rather surprised she hasn't called in a squad of psychologists."

"A city girl?"

"Very much so." He laughed. "I'm waiting to see how long it takes her and her chauffeur to venture down and see for herself what kind of fiasco I've gotten myself into."

## Chapter Seven

Angus didn't have to wonder for long. On Thursday the following week, Max was just heading out for a lunch break when a gleaming black limousine eased down the gravel drive. She guessed before the door opened it would have to be Angus's mother. A spit-shined chauffeur rushed to open the rear door as Max came down the stairs to greet her.

The petite blonde stood to look around, running a hand down her elegant slacks and straitening the cuffs of her cream-colored silk blouse. Max considered the contrast, rubbing her hands on her dusty jeans and moving forward, hoping that made them clean enough to be presentable.

"You must be Angus's mother," she said as she approached the car door.

The other woman slipped off her designer sunglasses to reveal brilliant blue eyes framed by mascara. "I am, darling. You may call me Lina." She gave her the once over, smiling. "And you must be Max."

That his mother knew her name surprised Max, but she tried not to let it show. "I am. Welcome to Angus's new home, such as it is."

She glanced at the porch, raising her eyebrows. "Well, it certainly looks homey."

Max stifled a chuckle. The house would hardly be what this elegant woman was accustomed to, but at least she had bothered to show some interest. "It'll be a lot more comfortable and stylish when we're finished." Angus appeared around the corner of the house, smiling.

"There's my darling boy." She stretched her arms out and he approached, bending down to hug her. Clearly, his height came from his father's side of the family.

"This is a nice surprise."

She laughed. "I had a whim to stage an ambush. Will you forgive me for interrupting your work?"

"It can wait." He kissed her cheek. "I see you've already met Max. Why don't we give you the grand tour?"

Max stayed out of the way while Angus led Lina around, introducing her to Nate and one of the drywallers. The other workmen had already left for lunch. Mother and son ended up gazing out at the back pasture. "What are you going to do with all of this space?" his mother asked, sounding perplexed.

"I'm going to adopt a dog when the house is finished and maybe put in a pool. I haven't decided for sure."

"Can you hire someone to mow all of that grass? It's actually a field, isn't it? I can't really tell."

He laughed. "I'm going to buy a riding mower. It's not a big deal. An hour or two on the weekend should take care of it."

"So, you haven't changed your mind yet?" Max thought she detected a hopeful note in Lina's question.

Angus shook his head. "It still feels like the right choice for me."

"I hope you're not offended," Lina said, directing the comment to Max. "He just made such a speedy decision."

"Not at all." She shrugged. "Some folks are country people, and some are city. That's reality."

"It's just I really thought he was the latter. He's lived in cities all his life."

Max sensed a little sadness there. "He said you were the best mom ever invented, so maybe it was you who made it right for him, not all of the hustle and bustle."

"What a sweet thing to say." She put a hand on Max's arm. "Do you have time to share lunch with us?"

The invitation caught her by surprise. "Oh, I wouldn't want to interrupt your time together."

"The more the merrier." Lina turned to look at Angus. "What's the best restaurant in town?"

Twenty minutes later, they were seated in a booth at Bo's. Lina's sole comment had been "Oh, my," and Max struggled not to giggle. The limousine had caused quite a stir, inspiring the rather introverted Bo to make an appearance. He stared at the beautiful car, muttered "Cool wheels," then retreated to the kitchen. Lina ordered a salad and winced when Max and Angus ordered burgers and fries. "I guess you need extra energy for all of the physical work you do."

Max nodded. "I usually have a salad at night, though. It helps balance things out."

"Salads are for an appetizer before the real meal," Angus responded, his eyes twinkling.

His mother sighed. “Men. They’re hopeless.” She took a dainty sip of her water. “How did you get into the construction business, Max?”

She repeated what she had told Angus on the weekend.

“That’s fascinating,” Lina replied. “Do you have any problems with men who are unwilling to obey orders from a woman?”

“No,” Max replied with a smile. “They just get fired.”

“Good for you.” She gave a little clap of approval. “Men don’t like to be kept in line, but the capacity to do so would be essential in your business. Have you had to fire many people?”

Max shook her head. “Only a few, thank goodness. I had to fire one recently, though. I hired a security guard for the house after he left until we finished. Apparently, he cruised by at night a couple of times, looking to stir up trouble.”

That caught Angus’s attention. “What did he do to get fired?”

“Showed up late almost daily and then did sub-standard work we had to redo.” She shrugged. “It happens. I’m lucky, though. Most of my crew have been with me for years.”

When their meals arrived, Lina appeared surprised by the fresh, colorful salad. “Oh, it looks lovely.”

“We’ve never had a bad meal here so far. Bo knows his stuff.” In between bites, Max said, “What was Angus like as a child?”

Lina sent him an adoring glance. “He lived with his head in a book, always banging into the furniture. His hair on the back of his neck stood at strange angles all of the time, because he was forever leaning against things while he read."

Angus's face flushed.

"What, no sports?" Max said, teasing.

Lina laughed. "Basketball coaches were always chasing after him because of his height. He made an attempt to join in to keep his father happy, but he was miserable. The same result with football and baseball."

"I like to hike," he said.

"You like to hike so you can find a better place to read," his mother replied with a giggle. "But he loves old movies, too, and that's certainly a point in his favor."

"You're kidding," Max said. "Who are your favorite actors?"

Angus finished his bite of burger and grabbed a french fry. "Jimmy Stewart, Rock Hudson, Katherine Hepburn…I could go on, but you get the gist."

"Have you seen *North by Northwest*?"

He looked surprised. "Love it. How about *Guess Who's Coming to Dinner*?"

"Oh, my goodness," Lina replied. "That one was considered quite scandalous back in my day." She beamed. "Old movie buffs. I love it. There aren't enough of us around."

They finished their meals, calling goodbye to Bo as they exited. Lina dropped them off at the house and headed back to Louisville. By the expression on Angus's face, she could see he was disappointed his mother didn't stay longer. "Give her a chance to get used to it."

"Who are you, Omar, the mind reader?" he said.

Max smiled. "I think she liked it more than expected. Wait until the house is done, then invite her for an overnight stay." She moved toward the house, then stopped. "You really adore her, don't you?"

His smile reflected in his eyes. "I do. She never cared that I was different from the other kids. She just let me be myself. There's no better gift to give a child." With those rather profound words, he headed around the corner to return to his trailer.

Max thought about what he'd said at three the next morning as she lay on the couch, patting the dogs as they slept. What would it have been like to have that kind of love growing up? She didn't envy much in this world, but she envied those who still had loving parents. Her adored mother had died when she was ten. Her father deserted them a few years before that and had subsequently passed on. She often wondered if she would have safely made it to adulthood without Nate. He made the nearly eight year stay in the orphan's home bearable. No one volunteered to adopt a child with her issues. Who could blame them?

That was why Angus's parting words had struck her. What a blessed gift to be allowed to develop as you wanted, without judgement or condemnation. If she ever had kids, at this date likely from a sperm bank, she would give them the gift of acceptance.

*Where did that thought come from?* The idea of children had seemed impossible for years. How do you explain a mother who can't sleep at night? And what if she passed this phobia on to her offspring?

Despite the psychological nature of her illness, she remained a practical person in every other way.

Because of that, she went to her stack of movies and picked out one to distract her.

You couldn't beat Katherine Hepburn and Sidney Poitier.

****

The watcher sat, observing Max eating a late dinner, his back shoved against the rough bark of a nearby tree. He didn't appreciate that Max seemed to like her new customer so much. What was the big deal about him? He wouldn't last a year out here in the country. He'd never be one of them.

At least she still retreated to her house every night so they could have their time together. From seven to eleven every night, like clockwork, barring illness or other responsibilities. He depended on it as if it was the air that filled his lungs.

Last week, that stupid chunk of a horse had wandered over to sniff him and he'd slapped him away with the flail of one hand. He would only put up with the animals because of her. She made his sacrifice worth it. If not for her, he would have killed the smelly bastards years ago so he wouldn't have to work to avoid them all the time. A few well-placed shots from a rifle would do it.

A while later, he glanced at his watch, pressing the knob to light up its face. He shook his head, surprised to see that it was already time to head home. Sometimes, the hours seemed to disappear without a trace. Standing to stretch, he blew her a kiss and headed back through the thicket of trees to his truck.

****

It made for an oddly intimate experience, living close to someone you didn't know well. Angus shifted on the undersized couch, almost dislodging the book he had propped on his chest to take a break from reading. Setting it on the end table, he stood and wandered to the small refrigerator, pouring himself a glass of milk.

He had a submission to finish for a scientific journal but found himself distracted by thoughts of Max. She intrigued him. Strong, smart, and funny had always been a winning combination for him, but she had something extra. A detail-oriented person, he couldn't figure out the reason behind his interest. Yes, she attracted him, but so had other women in the past.

The fact they were neighbors complicated the situation. If he pursued her and the relationship fell apart, wouldn't that just define awkward. As a fervent believer of the pro and con list, he compiled a mental version. The pros were that they had intelligence and a sense of humor in common, were both single, and liked each other's company. The cons were the neighbor thing and her fears. What caused them, and exactly how bad were they?

Angus came to a decision before he fell asleep. He would invite her to watch a movie with him and see how she reacted. If she looked horrified, he would have his answer, and if she just seemed flustered, he would consider her response encouraging data.

Around noon the next day, he watched the guys leave for lunch. Shortly afterward, Max ventured onto the rear porch and sat with her back propped against the wall. Grabbing a soda from his refrigerator, he wandered over. Her eyes were closed, and he stood still, wondering if she could have fallen asleep so quickly. He didn't want to wake her.

"I'm not asleep," she said.

"I can leave," he offered. "Lunch hour might be a great time to catch up on your sleep."

She opened her eyes, wincing at the sun and changing position to combat it. "Thankfully, I don't need much sleep. I'm trying to work out a problem before Nate shows up this afternoon."

"Maybe I can help." Angus dropped down to sit on the steps, taking a sip of his soda to give her a minute. Problem solving came easily to him compared with everything else.

She sighed. "I'm pretty sure I saw Nate's ex-wife in town this morning."

"She doesn't live here?"

"No."

"Oh, that's right. You said she took off, looking for more adventure. So, she showed up and you don't want to be the bearer of bad news."

"Exactly."

He took a moment to consider. "Perhaps she's just visiting family."

Max shook her head. "Her old man's in prison and her mother lives in Mexico."

"Do you think she's angling for a reconciliation?"

She laughed, but he detected the layer of scorn underneath. "She can try all she likes, but there is zero chance of that. Nate would never be so foolish as to make that mistake again. But she causes trouble everywhere she goes. Whatever her reason for being here, it won't be good."

"Maybe she just wants to spend time with Emma."

"That's what worries me. Sherisse won't just want to see Emma. She'll want to use her, somehow. It's what she does. She's a manipulator."

Angus nodded. "I guess we'll just have to see how it plays out and figure out how to best protect her."

She wondered at his use of the word, 'we,' but her answer was interrupted by the sound of wheels on gravel and the following thump of a door. Max leaned to peek through the open windows at the front. "Well, damn. Of all days to be early, Nate." She stood up with a groan.

"I'll give you guys some space." He came to his feet and watched her proceed through the doorway, hearing, "Thanks, Angus," as he walked away.

When he checked in at the house later, Nate's thunderous expression spoke volumes. He left shortly afterward to pick Emma up, his truck tires spitting some gravel as he left.

"That's the first time I've ever seen him angry," he said to Max.

She put down some drawings on the work bench, rubbing her neck. "It doesn't happen very often. He's a good-tempered guy." She sighed. "I didn't have to tell him after all. Apparently, the world's worst mother showed up at school recess and made a scene while the kids were playing in the yard. Thank goodness, the teacher is a friend who knows the story and shooed her away."

"He needs to see what she wants and then consult an attorney if necessary."

She nodded. "I agree."

He considered what he knew about the story. "You said this woman abandoned her at one and hasn't seen her since?" He thought about the typical scenario in cases like this. "Were there were drugs and alcohol involved?"

"Yes. Both, although alcohol seemed to be the biggest issue."

"Unless she became a nun in the intervening years, his rights of custody should be safe."

"I hope so."

He gestured around the kitchen. "Are you finished for the day?"

"Just cleaning up."

He took the broom out of her hands. "Let me help." They worked together, throwing out the scraps of leftover wood and sweeping the sawdust into a dustpan. "You keep a clean worksite."

"The guys tease me, but it reduces the chance of someone having an accident." She dumped the last few scraps in the waste barrel. "I appreciate the help."

"No problem. Why don't you go home and grab some rest? I imagine Nate will be showing up looking for some advice before too long."

She tilted her head. "You're kind of a caretaker soul, aren't you?"

Her comment surprised him. "I never really thought of it that way," he said. "I'm just efficient." He watched as she slapped the dust off her jeans. "But if there's any way I can help, let me know."

He ate his dinner feeling like a martyr, forcing the healthy salad down his throat to make amends for other less-prudent meals. Hiking across his back pasture in the mornings had helped a bit. He reminded himself to buy a few hand weights. Gyms were made for gregarious people, and the bulging biceps group depressed him. He just wanted to stay fit, not look like a cartoon character. He didn't hear much from next door and wondered what difficulties Nate might be facing.

## Chapter Eight

The following day, it poured rain from sunrise to nightfall. By noon, he'd grown bored of writing his paper and sick of the four walls closing in. He escaped to the house, risking booming thunder and occasional dramatic spears of lightning for an ungainly three-minute dash with a garbage bag held over his head. As he shook himself off on the back porch, he caught sight of Max and Nate grinning at him through the window. They opened the sliding door for him. "Not your best look, friend," Nate offered.

He laughed. "Guess I'd better buy a raincoat."

"And boots," Max added, pointing to his sneakers, which were now coated up to the laces in mud.

"Shoot," he said, slipping them off to leave them outside on the porch, not wanting to track up the house.

After he joined them inside, Nate threw him a dry pair, and he saw with surprise they would only be a little big. "Thanks."

"No problem. We learned a long time ago to keep dry spares handy."

Angus pushed his damp hair out of his eyes. "I didn't even realize you guys were here."

Max shrugged, raising her voice to be heard over a sudden tattoo of rain blowing against the windows. "It's too wet to finish the drywall, but we thought we would finalize the ideas on your built-ins. Do you want to have a look?"

The drawings were slightly amended but had much more detail. He could see it in his mind. The rich, golden brown stain they proposed fit his taste, and he gave everything a thumbs up. Afterward, they looked at her recommendations for furniture. Other than a change on one chair, he loved all the pieces Max had chosen and gave them his approval so they could go ahead and order them. He knew not all construction firms offered design assistance, so he told them how much he appreciated the extra help.

"So far, we figure you're the easiest client we've ever had. Most people second-guess us into an early grave."

He smiled. "It's selfish, really. I don't want to be the reason we don't finish on schedule."

"That's fair, as long as you get everything exactly the way you want it." She rolled up the plans and set them in an empty corner of the room. "We're going to brave the elements and treat ourselves to lunch at Bo's. Want to come?"

"Absolutely."

They bundled into Nate's truck, getting a break from the rain that lasted just long enough for them to dash into the restaurant. Only half of the seats were occupied, a testament to the cranky weather. All three ordered burgers and splurged on shakes. Halfway through, Nate's demeanor changed when the front bell rang to announce another patron. Angus faced away from the door, but he knew who had come in from reading the other man's expression. Max put a hand on his wrist and, suddenly, a petite, curvy blonde came into view.

"My, my. Isn't this cozy." The buxom woman certainly had looks to tempt, but the tone of her voice implied less than friendly intention. "As usual, Max is grabbing more than her fair share of men, even if they belong to someone else."

"Go away, Sherisse," Nate said. "Find another fool to prey on."

She fluffed her hair, thrusting her chest forward, in a gesture likely practiced for years. Batting her artistically shadowed eyes, she focused on Angus. "Oh, I don't know. I heard your friend is a pretty big fish for this podunk pond."

Angus met her gaze. "Thanks, but Nate and I are pretty happy sharing Max's company." He heard Max strangling a laugh. "But be sure to enjoy your short visit in town."

Her lips receded from her teeth, the way a wolverine threatens their enemy. Angus found it fascinating to watch the metamorphosis. "I might decide to move back and reunite with my beloved daughter."

"She doesn't even know who you are," Max scorned. "Good luck with that."

"She's my daughter, not yours. You can't tell me what to do," the other woman shot back, her voice escalating.

Bo's head and neck popped through the kitchen door, searching for the source of the raised voices. After a pause, his sturdy body followed. He stood, braced, his arms folded across his chest. "Take off, Sherisse. We don't need your kind of trouble here."

The woman turned on her heel and flounced away. Bo laughed, a hooting sound, when she tried, and failed, to slam the glass door. "Good riddance to bad rubbish," he said, before disappearing into the kitchen.

They stayed silent as they finished their meals.

"Can I offer some advice?" Angus asked.

Nate nodded.

"Take notes on every confrontation, on every single word she says to you, Emma, or your friends. That way, if it goes to court, you can show a continuing pattern of bad behavior."

Looking impressed, Nate said, "That's a great idea."

"If I read her right, I'd say what she's looking for is likely money, rather than a loving relationship." He met the other man's eyes. "Even if you're tempted to pay her off, don't do it. If you do, you'll be bled dry for the rest of your life."

Nate paused. "I appreciate it, Angus. Do you have any ideas on who to pick if we need a lawyer?"

"Don't worry. If it comes to that, I know people who can help."

****

The next two days passed without incident, and Max dared to feel some relief. She and Nate had been extra careful with Emma, watching her every move. On the third day, however, Sherisse showed up at the worksite, dressed in a blouse which could barely contain her considerable assets and a skirt scarcely long enough to deserve the name. She strolled in the door, and all the machines stopped as the men who didn't know her gawked.

"Get back to work," Max ordered, and they did. She walked up to the other woman. "Sherisse, this is a job site. You have to leave."

"Where's Nate?"

"He's not here."

Sherisse smirked. "That's funny. His truck is parked out front." She tried to peek around her. "Where ya hidin', sweetie?"

Nate's voice sounded from the back of the house. "You want to talk to me, get out here." He came out from the other room and pointed through the open door to the porch.

His ex-wife gave a mock shiver. "Ooh, I love it when you talk rough." She sashayed past the men, rubbing a hand over her butt as she passed.

Max followed, shutting the door behind her for the illusion of privacy. She moved to stand next to Nate.

"I didn't ask you to join us," Sherisse spat, taking an unplanned step that made her teeter on her high heels.

Max smiled. "Nate did, though."

His face turned red. "What do you want, Sherisse?"

"I want to see my daughter." She sauntered across to him, running her hands up his shirtfront.

He stepped away from the contact. "Why now?"

"What do you mean?" Her wide-eyed play at innocence made a mockery of it.

He rubbed his face, and Max recognized the attempt to control his temper. "You haven't come near her for five years and, all of a sudden, you need to see her?"

She grinned, her fangs showing. “Well, I’ve turned my life around. I think I’d like to try my hand at motherhood.”

“Not gonna happen.”

“That’s not what my lawyer says.”

Max could read the enjoyment the woman got out of the shock on Nate’s face. “Clearly, your lawyer doesn’t know about your past behavior,” she replied, to give Nate time to recover.

The other woman whirled toward her and advanced. “It’s none of your business, bitch. You obviously didn’t listen to what I said in the diner. She’s my child, not yours.”

“Max has been more of a mother to Emma than you ever have.” Nate took an audible breath. “You need to leave. Now. I have full custody, and I have no intention of letting you see Emma.”

Sherisse pivoted to face him, her expression making a joke of her previous guise. “You’ll regret it, Nate.” She clasped her hands in front of her, softening her expression into martyrdom. “I only left because I was so scared of you. You’re one big, awful man against poor little me.” She gave a mock shudder. “It’ll work, you know. Who’s going to believe a man with a record against all this?” Sweeping a hand up and down her body, she added, “You might want to rethink your limited options.”

Turning on her heel, she stormed through the house, kicking the garbage can on the way out. Trash spilled everywhere. After a moment, they heard the angry growl of an engine pushed too hard and moved to the front of the house to see her compact car skidding down the drive.

Nate groaned. "You got any paper around?"

Confused, Max said, "What?"

"Remember what Angus said. We should write all of her bullshit down."

"Oh, yeah," she replied. "Let's go borrow some from him. He's working."

They traipsed across the lawn and rapped on his door. He answered with what she thought of as his doctor glasses on. "Come in."

"We don't want to interrupt," Max offered. "Sherisse just caused a disturbance, and we need to note every word, like you suggested."

"Sit. I was planning to break for lunch, anyway." He let them all get settled as he rummaged for several sheets of paper and a pen. "How bad was it?"

Nate related the gist to him as Max wrote it down.

Angus frowned when they came to the part about his record. "If you don't mind me asking, what were you jailed for?"

Max jumped in. "He defended his mother. His father took his anger out on him instead and smashed a bottle against his face."

*Hence, the scar*. "Sorry, but how did his behavior lead to charges for you?"

Poor Nate brushed away the sweat running down his face. "There's no record. The charges were dropped. My father tried to say I attacked him with no provocation, but he didn't know Max was watching through the window." He attempted a smile. "Thank goodness."

"Well, it shouldn't matter, then."

"She can still make me look like a hothead."

Max snorted. “And you have dozens of people who would say the exact opposite, including the police chief. People who would testify, if needed.” She sighed. “Do you think we should call a lawyer now?”

“I have a friend who owes me a favor. Why don’t you let me contact him, and I’ll relay this information? That way, he can give us some advice on how to proceed.”

“Does this guy know his stuff?” Nate asked.

Angus smiled. “He’s the most successful lawyer specializing in custody issues in the state.”

“Geez, Angus. I can’t afford to consult someone like that.”

“He’s an old friend from my university days. The phone call will be a freebie. After that, we can figure out what’s what.” He reached for his cellphone and raised his eyebrows. “Fair game?”

Nate sighed. “I really appreciate it.”

Max and Nate listened to a one-sided conversation as Angus outlined the details. After that, his side consisted mostly of “yes”, “no,” and “that’s what I thought.” After fifteen minutes, he hung up. “Here’s the gist. My friend agrees she is likely after money, and it’s important you let her get to the point of asking for it.”

“Why?” Nate asked.

“Because that’s when you gain the upper hand. Once you prove her primary goal is money, the request and her history will sink her ambitions.”

“They won’t believe me.”

“That may be true.” He shrugged. “But if you had someone with a sterling reputation who would testify to her blackmail, that would do it.”

“They would just say Max lied to protect me.”

Angus laughed. "I meant me. I've testified in a dozen court cases through the years."

"Oh." Nate drummed his fingers on the arm of the chair. "Couldn't we just record her?"

Angus shook his head. "Recordings are being questioned a lot more than they used to be, because they are easy to tamper with."

"What if you're not around at the right time? It seems a little chancy to me."

"You'd have to play it carefully, so she asks for the money in a place you control. Maybe your house. She would never know I sat in a back room, working, with the door cracked open."

Max cocked her head, considering. "You're a little devious, aren't you, underneath all of your professor stuff?"

"Yes." He took off his computer glasses and polished them with the edge of his shirt. "In academia, you better stay on top of your game or someone else walks off with your career."

It gave her a new perspective on her neighbor, and she really appreciated how he always seemed so ready to help. "Right now, I feel we should celebrate having a plan in place for this by going to Bo's for lunch. My treat."

****

Ian showed up at the worksite the next morning. Angus had just joined Max and Nate. They were all checking out the newly finished drywall which allowed them to imagine the rooms better. "Holy smokes," Ian said, gesturing as he wandered around, taking in the changes. "It looks like a whole new house already."

“That’s the point,” Max replied with a grin. “Did you think I was just spending your pal’s money for kicks?”

He shook his head. “Nah, but, damn it, now this house makes my place look like a dog kennel.” Walking into the kitchen, he said, “I can already see our master chef cookin’ up a storm in here.”

“How are the bad guys treating you?” Nate asked.

Ian frowned. “Had to arrest a guy for beatin’ his kid last night. I hate that shit.” He rolled his eyes. “Then I went to have a beer with some of the guys and guess who was there?”

“The girl of your dreams?” Angus suggested.

He snorted. “Not hardly. It was Sherisse.”

“Of course, she’ll be busy spreading her venom,” Max replied, patting Nate’s arm. “She came here to gift us with her presence yesterday.”

“Well, she pranced on in there, shakin’ her money maker as if she owned the place. The only guys who went near her are the drunks and the ones who don’t know her.” He sighed. “She’s real pretty until she opens her mouth.”

Max laughed. “Well put.”

He turned to Nate. “The only reason I dropped by is that it seems like she’s trying to stir up trouble for you. I thought I’d better warn you before I forgot.”

“No doubt about that, I’m afraid. What did she do?”

“She started talking about your supposed record and how you aren’t a fit father. Then she was askin’ how often you’re drinkin’ these days.” He shook his head. “The stupid thing is she drank like a fish the whole time. I kept hoping she’d try to drive home so I could arrest her, but no such luck. She convinced some dumbass to drive her back to her hotel."

"We'll write it all down." At Ian's confused look, Max explained their plan.

Ian nodded. "That's a great idea. And I'll keep my eyes open." He gave Nate a friendly slap on the back. "Don't worry. She doesn't have a clue how many friends you have around here. She won't get away with any crap."

"I hope you're right."

He said his goodbyes, and they all returned to work. Angus had finally finished his paper and was slaving over a final edit before sending it off to his favorite scientific journal. He sat under the canopy, marking notes in red along the margins of his hard copy.

He looked up just in time to catch Max heading home at day's end and waved her over.

She glanced at his paper as he patted the dogs. "What are you doing?"

"I just finished my paper, so I'm doing a final edit." He paused, thinking, well, here goes. "Do you want to watch an old movie with me tomorrow night?" She looked shocked, so he gave her a moment.

"Here?" she stuttered.

Chuckling, he nodded. "What? My fancy trailer isn't good enough for you and the dogs?"

She took a step back, shaking her head. "I don't go out at night."

"I can walk you home afterward."

"Angus," she said, "I don't do that kind of thing."

He forced a look of puzzlement onto his face. "You don't watch movies with Nate and other friends?"

She peered at him, brushing the bangs out of her eyes, the first time he had seen her less than confident. "With Nate?"

"Sure," he answered, as if that had been his plan all along. "We could watch a movie and let Emma have a sleepover. It's been an exhausting week. We could all use some relaxation."

The stress left her eyes. "I guess that might be fun. Why don't we do it at my place though? The bigger kitchen means we can lay out some snack food."

"Sure. So, would tomorrow night work?"

"I'll check with Nate, but it should be fine. If it's not, I'll let you know tonight."

Angus smiled. "Sounds good." Max turned and left. He watched her climb the slope to her place.

He spent the rest of the evening hoping the phone wouldn't ring. Her agreement meant one small step in the right direction. He wasn't greedy, he would take it. When the phone stayed quiet, he went to sleep, content.

## Chapter Nine

The great thing about Saturdays was that they usually offered an opportunity for Max to catch up on rest. She'd fallen asleep as the sun rose and slept until after eleven, a long time for her. Refreshed, she found herself looking forward to the evening, although she was a little embarrassed she had thought Angus meant a date.

It made her wonder what he liked to do on dates. Well, besides the obvious, of course. He was a man, after all.

Chasing down the laundry basket, she threw a load of dirty clothes into the washer. She must be getting senile. She could have sworn she left the damn basket in her bedroom. And she couldn't find either of her favorite shirts. Shrugging, she decided they'd turn up sooner or later.

After Max ate, she texted the guys about food for tonight. Nate said, "Whatever," which was typical. Angus, on the other hand, texted:

*—I'll take care of it. Can I come thirty minutes early and use your stove?—*

She answered in the affirmative, wondering what he had planned. After spending a relaxing few hours taking a ride on Ghost, she shampooed the dogs. They were a little fragrant after diving into muddy water as they followed her through the woods. Nate and Emma had gone to a school fair for the afternoon.

At six-thirty on the dot, a knock sounded on the door. Max shoved the dogs away and looked through the peephole to find Angus waiting, his arms full. She opened the door to admit him, and the dogs swarmed as he lifted two grocery bags away from their insistent noses. "Down," she insisted. They hit the floor, wiggling, and he stepped over them.

"Good heavens. It looks like you brought enough for an army."

He set his haul down on the counter. "I take food pretty seriously, but this stuff is easy."

"I hope I have everything you need." She gestured to the cabinets, thinking that if he needed any specialty items, they were sunk.

He grinned. "Don't worry. Two or three large spoons plus a casserole dish and we're good to go."

"I have those, for sure." She pulled each one out, setting them on the counter, and received his nod of approval.

"Now, I have a confession to make," he said, rubbing his hands together. "I'm very territorial when I work in the kitchen. Could you stand on the other side of the island? That way, I can move around without worrying about stepping on your toes."

"Small price to pay for free food." She scurried to the other side and observed as he emptied the bags, his hands moving efficiently between items. "So, you're a bit of a control freak?"

"Guilty." He set the temperature on the oven. "Oh, I forgot. I need a cutting board and knife, too."

Pointing to their location, she laughed. “You really do enjoy this, don’t you?”

He nodded as he chopped an onion. “It’s a little sexist of you to be so surprised,” he joked. “A lot of scientists like to cook. It’s the whole idea of precision and experiments, I guess.”

“That makes sense.” She watched him pull out a package of bacon, her favorite. “Hmmm. What are you making with that?”

“Blue cheese and figs wrapped in bacon and then broiled. They’ll keep everybody content until dinner is ready.”

“And what’s the main dish?”

“It’s a surprise.”

She watched, entranced. “I realized maybe we should have invited Ian, too.”

“It’s okay. I checked earlier. He has to cover a shift for one of his men tonight.”

“He’ll hate that. He always tries to avoid working on any night, much less Saturday.”

“I can’t blame him for that. It’s one of the main reasons he wanted to be in charge.” Angus pulled a bottle of wine and a corkscrew out of one bag. “Do you want some?”

She nodded, pointing to the upper cupboard which contained the glasses. “I’ll open and pour, so you can keep working.”

“Sounds good.” He placed wine, glasses, and the opener on the counter in front of her. “Anyway, I think it might be beneficial for Ian to miss a few Saturday nights. He still has lousy taste in women.”

She burst out laughing. Popping the cork and pouring each of them a glass, she said, “I’m glad Nate and I aren’t the only ones who think so.”

As if summoned by his name, Nate came through the back door with Emma. She rushed across the room, clapping her hands. “Agnus, we’re gonna have movie night.”

Max smiled at her pronunciation. “It’s like Gus with An in front of it.”

Emma looked indignant. “That’s what I said, Max.”

“Close enough,” Angus said. “Do you want to be the food tester, Emma?”

“Yes!”

He turned toward Nate. “She doesn’t have any food allergies, does she?”

Nate patted his stomach. “Unfortunately, she’s just like her old man. She can, and will, eat everything in sight.”

The bacon munchies were a big hit. Emma carried them around on the plate, offering them to everyone, her cheeks bulging with the one she’d taken. Max sent the dogs to their beds in the corner, so she wouldn’t have to battle their noses every time food made an appearance. Everyone voted on their favorite movie, and they put on the first one while dinner finished cooking.

It didn’t seem at all strange to have Angus in her house, which surprised Max. He fit right in. On paper, you wouldn’t think he would, being far more educated than they were.

When they broke for dinner, she found the creamy chicken casserole delicious, the delicate taste of rosemary and oregano lingering on her tongue. "Who taught you how to cook? This is amazing."

"My mother's housekeeper, Anna. She's been with Mom for thirty years."

Max sighed. "Remind me to thank her."

Emma fell asleep around ten, and Nate carried her to the guest bedroom. Max collected her stuffed animals to place them around her. She looked like an angel with a halo of fluffy guardians to guard her. The three adults watched another movie until midnight and then Angus said goodnight, leaving a couple days of leftovers for Max to enjoy.

****

*Well, isn't that sweet.* He spat out the blade of grass he'd had between his teeth as he waited. Now, this jerk is spending the evening with her. He paced under the canopy of trees, cursing under his breath. Trying to calm himself down, he watched the egghead stroll back to his trailer as if he didn't have a care in the world.

He had to put a stop to this.

He'd been more than patient, his only indulgence an occasional foray inside her house while the dogs played outside and she'd gone to work. Last time, he'd left the laundry basket in the wrong place, but she hadn't seemed to notice or mention anything. The clothing he borrowed carried her scent. He placed it under his pillow so he could fall asleep dreaming of her.

She was his forever girl. She just didn't know it yet. And anyone who tried to interfere with their future might find themselves on the receiving end of a death warrant.

****

On Monday morning, Max was walking to work when she saw Sherisse's car pulling into Nate's driveway, a harbinger of bad things to come. She sent a warning text to him, so he'd be prepared. "Do you need me to come?" she texted. He replied in the negative.

A few minutes later, Angus stuck his head in the door. He waited while she checked in with the men who were working. She walked over to the back door where he stood. "Hey."

"Nate's got a visitor."

She nodded. "I know. I texted to warn him, but he said he was okay."

They didn't have to wait long to find out what she wanted. Nate showed up in the backyard, waving them to join him, away from prying ears. His flushed face and frown told the story. "She brought some lowlife lawyer wearing a cheap suit who served me with papers. They're suing me for custody of Emma."

Angus put hand on his arm. "Did you get the lawyer's name?"

Nate handed him a business card. "I thought this guy was a lowlife ambulance chaser."

"He might be." Angus paused to consider the possibilities. "Is there any chance she is using a…personal relationship to avoid legal fees?"

"Oh, yeah." Nate gave a bitter smile. "He couldn't take his eyes off her."

Max swore, exhausted by all of her disgusting manipulations.

Angus smiled. "No, that's a good thing, Nate. If she's not paying him in cash and it's not his normal type of legal practice, those are two big advantages."

"How so?" Nate asked.

"He'll be operating on unfamiliar ground. If we have to pull out our big gun, he'll panic when he checks him out." He met the other man's gaze. "I'll ask my friend for advice, but I'd bet if we just give him my contact's card and tell them to send any paperwork to him, that's when a cash demand will come."

For the first time in recent days, a hopeful expression crossed Nate's face. "It could happen that quick? Do you really think so?"

Angus shrugged. "It probably won't be tomorrow, but I bet it won't be long. She's not the patient sort, is she?"

"Hell, no."

"You just have to make sure you don't talk to her without me hiding in your back room."

Nate rubbed his hands over his face. "Do you have any work trips coming up?"

"No. Not for the next two weeks. Personally, I don't think there's any way she'll last more than a few days." He moved towards the door. "Why don't I let you guys get back to work? We can talk about this tonight."

They clustered around Max's kitchen table that night, making plans. They would all stay close to home for the next week, expecting something to break. When Sherisse called to set up a meeting, Nate would insist it take place at his house. Angus would go and hang out in Nate's spare bedroom, the closest room to the kitchen.

Thanks to the demands of his job, Angus had developed an amazing memory, but he would take notes to try and record every word. They all agreed they wouldn't confront her at that point, but Nate's job would be to make sure the clear wording spelled it out—money in lieu of her child.

They spent the next stressful week working hard and waiting for some kind of progress. Nate delivered the lawyer's business card to Sherisse on Monday with instructions to forward the paperwork to him. The fact she didn't show up soon afterward made them all question whether they were right about her intentions.

But Friday, the tide changed. First thing in the morning, Sherisse asked Nate for a meeting that night. She asked him to meet him at the bar she preferred, but he insisted it be at his home. He came over to the job site after the call and told them. "My hands were actually shaking," he admitted with evident embarrassment. "I don't think I'm cut out for this kind of thing."

Max gestured to Angus. "It's as if he has a crystal ball or something."

Angus shook his head. "No. It's just the best predictor of future behavior is past behavior. Nate told me she has always been money-hungry."

"That's something to be grateful for, I guess."

"What time is she coming?" Angus asked.

"Six p.m." He frowned. "She's probably planning a night of celebration afterward."

"Okay," Angus said. "Put a nice comfortable chair close to the bedroom door and I'll come over at five, in case she tries to surprise you by arriving early." He smiled. "And we can have our own celebration afterward."

"I'll buy everyone a night on the town if this works," Nate said.

Max nodded. "It sounds like a great plan. Just drop Emma off at her friend's place right after school. She'll be out of the picture, and you guys should be all set." She groaned. "I'll have every body part I can manage crossed for good luck."

That evening, she waited at home, trying not to bite her nails. A lot of 'what if' scenarios cluttered her mind. *What if it didn't work?*

*What if Sherisse gets even partial custody rights?*

*What if Angus is wrong about her asking for money?* So much depended on this one conversation.

She wanted to join Angus in the back room, but he insisted they had to keep the plan as streamlined as possible. If it ever came to court, Angus would simply say Nate had lent him the back room to work in and he had overheard the conversation. But Angus doubted it would ever go that far. *Is he right?* She could hardly bear the suspense.

Sherisse's car entered Nate's driveway early, at five-thirty. Max texted to warn the two of them and guarantee Angus had hidden out of sight. After that, all she could do was wait and pray for divine intervention.

## Chapter Ten

Angus heard the front door creak open and Nate's grudging invitation to enter. Footsteps scraped down the floorboards in the hall. "Let's sit in the den and get comfy," Sherisse chirped, clearly enjoying the situation.

"We're not here to get comfortable. I'm set up in the kitchen." Angus saw the flicker of Nate's shadow through the crack in the open door as he pulled out a chair and sat.

The click of high heels followed him. "Where are your manners, Nate? You don't pull a chair out for a lady anymore?"

"I don't see any lady here."

She dragged her chair out and sat. Angus could see the tip of one shoe, which started to bounce in a restless manner. "Where's my beautiful baby?" she said.

"Emma's with friends."

"Who, your bitch neighbor?"

"None of your business." He cleared his throat. "Why are you here, anyway? We have nothing to talk about."

The tone of her voice changed, as if she had adjusted a knob on the manipulation scale. "You had to sick a big, fancy lawyer on me. That's not playing fair, Nate."

"What would you know about fair? You're the one who's pretending to be a mother when you haven't even tried to see Emma in five years."

"Things have changed. I've turned over a new leaf."

Nate snorted, derision powering the sound. "Like hell you have. You don't give a damn about our daughter. You never did."

"I only want what's best for her. And the way things are lookin' that might be me."

"What's best for Emma is for you to crawl back to whatever hole you escaped from and leave us in peace." The terse words demonstrated his frustration.

In the pause, Angus scribbled on his pad, making notes to be sure he remembered every word.

She gave a breathy sigh. "I could say I came here to talk and you hit me. You have a reputation for that kind of thing."

"Don't threaten me, Sherisse. My reputation is sterling in this community, which is more than I can say for yours." Angus could hear the rising anger in Nate's words and wished he could send him a telepathic message to stay calm.

"Who are they going to believe, Nate? Innocent little me or a great hulking brute with a violent past."

"I'll take my chances on the legal system. It's time for you to leave. All this back and forth is getting us nowhere."

Don't rush her, Angus thought, hoping his friend hadn't pushed too soon. He held his breath, waiting, straining to hear her response.

"Oh, Nate. You always were impatient. There's another solution, you know."

The breath stuck in Angus's throat. *Oh, please, for Nate's sake, let this be the shakedown. Come on.* He didn't know how long his friend could hold his temper.

"What are you talking about?" Angus heard just the right level of irritation in Nate's voice. "What solution?"

"I have a lot of expenses, you know. It's not easy for a poor, single woman like me to have the high-quality life I deserve." The shadows in the kitchen shifted and Angus could picture her, leaning over to bat her eyes. "A little cold, hard cash might convince me to change my mind about all of this."

*Bingo.* Angus clenched his pen, hoping she would get more specific.

"What do you mean?" Nate said.

"Well, you and Max are haulin' in a lot of cash for yourselves from what I hear. A measly hundred thousand dollars wouldn't kill you. Consider it an investment in my future."

Nate's chair ground against the floor as he shoved it back. "So, that's the price you put on your daughter's head. A hundred thousand dollars."

She chuckled. "Oh, I'd say a million, of course, but a girl has to be realistic." Her tone turned playful now, and it even made Angus mad.

"Get out." Nate jumped to his feet, a tiny piece of his side visible as his chair banged against the oven door.

The sound of Sherisse's heels scraped on the vinyl floor as she rose. "I'm sure you need some time to think about it. I'll drop by tomorrow." The pungent scent of cheap perfume wafted through the open door.

"I won't be here."

"Oh, I'll find you. If you're smart, you'll have that check ready and waiting." The sound of tapping heels receded, and Angus heard the door slam behind her. He didn't move until an engine revved and he could hear her car start down the drive, rattling the gravel. Opening the door wide, he entered the kitchen.

As expected, Nate looked like a group of turbulent clouds, ready to burst. "That conniving bitch."

"You did great. She gave us exactly the leverage we need." Angus reached past him into the refrigerator and handed the other man a beer, adding one for himself. They had just taken a gulp when Max yanked open the back door and entered.

"Did she do it?"

Angus nodded.

She ran over and hugged Nate. "I'm almost scared to ask. How much did she try for?"

When they told her, she added a few curses of her own, then leaned over and patted Angus's arm. "I can't believe it. You were right. I'm so glad you were around to advise us."

"Glad to be of service," Angus said, smiling.

"So, when do we tell her the gig is up?" Nate asked.

He shrugged. "I'd allow her to have her night of celebration because that will lower her guard. Then we can hit her with a dose of reality tomorrow. Let her track you down at the work site, and I'll be there, too."

"Sounds like a plan," Nate answered, taking a swig of his beer, his expression a lot more relaxed now. "It feels a little weird to think I should be happy about someone attempting to blackmail me."

He made them all turkey sandwiches, adding chips to the side. "This is enough of a gourmet meal for me," Max joked. They were all eating when Emma's friend's mother dropped her off. The little girl chattered nonstop until she fell asleep on the couch, next to Nate.

"Be right back," he said, lifting his daughter with care. He transferred her to her bedroom, and they could hear him close the door so they wouldn't wake her.

"The timing worked out perfectly," Angus commented. "I just found out I have to be away for a couple of days next week."

"Nerd emergency?" Max asked, grinning.

He nodded. "A university study an acquaintance has been working on for a year hit a major snag. He needs another set of eyes to sort out the problem. It shouldn't be a big deal."

"Where?"

"Louisville."

She smiled. "Your mom will be happy."

"I'll let her know tomorrow. It'll be good to see her."

About an hour after they finished dinner, Max stood to leave. Angus came to his feet. "I'll walk you back. I still have some work to do."

They strolled along the driveway, walking over to pat Ghost when he wandered up to the fence. "Poor Nate." Max sighed. "I think he hoped Sherisse would never come back."

They resumed walking. "I think she'll take off for parts unknown after he sets the record straight tomorrow. She's on the prowl for easy money, and she just picked the wrong mark this time." He considered the few similar women he'd met through the years.

"Women like her spend their entire lives attaching themselves to man after man, hoping to hit the motherload one day. Anything to avoid having to work for it like the rest of us do."

Max gaped. "That's the most cynical thing I've ever heard you say."

"Am I wrong?"

She laughed. "Nope. When it comes to Sherisse, and women like her, you're right on the money."

"I'm curious. What did he ever see in her, other than the obvious?"

"I think he just wanted to create a home for himself. He's a very monogamous person by nature, and she said all the right things to convince him that she fit the bill."

He paused as they approached her front door. "It must have been difficult for you to watch because I doubt she ever fooled you."

"That's pretty perceptive. I'm impressed." She pulled out her keys. "Nate and I didn't see eye to eye about her from the very beginning. She was never good enough for him. Not even close." She pushed her hair out of her eyes. "You know how it is. There are rare occasions in any relationship when you don't want to be right but know you are. Being a friend means not always taking the easy path."

"A profound truth if I've ever heard one." Patting her shoulder, he turned to leave.

"Angus?"

He turned back.

"Thanks for helping Nate and Emma."

He shrugged. "The good guys have to stick together, right?"

"That's true." She said goodnight, opened the door, and went inside.

****

Mid-afternoon the next day, Sherisse's car turned in the driveway. Max ran and alerted Angus so they were all gathered at the back of the house when she pranced her way inside.

"I have to talk to Nate," she announced, gesturing for them to leave with a dismissive flick of her hand.

Max crossed her arms. "We're not leaving." Angus stood silent beside her.

She bared her teeth like a spitting cat. "We have business to discuss, you uppity bitch. Business that's no concern of yours."

"Only you would consider blackmail business, Sherisse."

She raised her eyebrows, turning to Nate. "Of course, you had to open your big mouth and blab about our arrangement, running like a child to your mommy."

"You wouldn't know anything about mommies, would you?" He shook his head, disgust written on the pinched lines of his face.

Stamping one foot, she said, "I don't have to take your bullshit, Nate. You're the one who stands to lose everything you've worked for."

He gritted his teeth and Angus had to applaud his restraint. "Don't threaten me, Sherisse. Your trumped-up garbage didn't work last night, and it's not going to work today, either."

"I'll take her away from you and leave you with nothing." She spun around to face the others. "He threatened me last night. I guess I'll have to report that to the police."

Angus stepped forward. “He didn’t threaten you. You’re the one who tried to blackmail him.”

“No one will ever believe him!”

Angus noticed she didn’t deny it. He smiled. “They’ll believe me.”

“Fat lot of good that’ll do him. You weren’t there.”

“Would you like to place a wager on that?” He moved a step closer now he had her undivided attention. “I happened to be doing some paperwork in the back bedroom and overheard the entire conversation. I am more than happy to testify for Nate as to the nature of the discussion, including your attempted extortion.”

Her face turned red, her expression twisting into a sneer. Black mascara dripped like venom from her lashes. “You think you’re a big deal, don’t you?”

“Actually, I am a pretty big deal, Sherisse. Look me up.” He took a step toward her. “I am experienced in testifying in court and, this time in particular, it would be an absolute pleasure to testify against you.”

Sherisse shrieked, shoving by Nate and turning over a small ladder as she stormed away. They listened to the string of curses as she made her way through the front door, further maddened by the chuckling of the crew as she passed. Her car fishtailed as she roared off, skidding and almost clipping Nate’s truck on the way.

Angus sighed. “That was way more satisfying than I expected.”

“She’s lost whatever mind she had in the first place,” Max replied.

Nate turned from staring out the front door. “Do you think she’ll leave town now?”

Angus nodded. "I think so. I warned Ian she might try to spin a tale for his benefit, but he's prepared if she does." When he called his lawyer friend later to tell him the good news, he said congratulations and told them he already knew. Apparently, Sherisse's discount lawyer sent them an email saying they were dropping the case.

Later, they all went to Tony's for pizza, Nate's treat. Ian joined them, telling them Sherisse had indeed come by the station house. He talked around his first bite. "I corrected her version of events, then casually mentioned I'd heard your lawyer was expected in town tomorrow. Two hours later, my friend, who's the manager at her hotel, said she had returned in a lather, cursing everyone in her path. She checked out earlier than planned." He leaned forward to give Nate a high-five. "Case dismissed."

After dinner, Max, Nate, and Angus stood by Max's front door while Emma played with the dogs. "Want to come in? We could look over the final paint colors."

"Gotta take Em home," Nate said. "She has schoolwork to get done before bed." He called her and she came running. "Say goodnight, Em."

"Dad, can't we stay a little longer? Puhleeeze." Her eyes begging, she put her hands in prayer position.

He shook his head, pointing down the drive. "School night. Give Max a hug, and let's go."

She ran over and squeezed Max's leg and then ran to Angus. "Lean down, Agnus, so I can hug you."

He glanced at Nate, waiting for his nod of approval, which he received. He leaned over and she squeezed his neck while he patted her back. "Night, you two," Nate said, and they headed down the drive.

"You look smitten," Max said.

Angus smiled. "He's a lucky man. You couldn't conjure up a more perfect kid if you followed a recipe."

His comment made her smile. "Got a few spare minutes to look at paint samples?"

"Sure." He followed her into the house, and she waved him to a kitchen chair. She carried a stack of flat pieces of drywall over, and, surprised, he saw she had painted each of them one of the possible colors. "I expected to have to squint at those tiny paint samples from the hardware store."

She laughed. "I've found through the years that it's hard to pick a color from such a small sample. If you use one of these, you can prop it up, see exactly how the light hits it, and look at it at different times of the day."

"Great idea." He peered over her shoulder. "I kind of like the yellow you suggested for the kitchen, which surprises me."

"Good. I picked a nice, creamy yellow, so it's not too bright. It makes a nice contrast to the greens and browns."

He picked a rich cream and sage scheme for the rest of the house, choices with which she agreed. Suddenly, she stood up and flipped on all the house lights. He realized the sun had begun to set. Not wanting his time with her to end, he kept talking. "So, do we put these in the house tomorrow to make sure they're what I want?"

She nodded. "Yes. Hopefully, they still look acceptable to you at the end of the day. If they do, the painters will get them mixed at the store the following morning so they can start painting."

"I can't believe with all of this drama you still kept the job on track. I'm really impressed."

"Thanks. You have to be flexible in this business. Weird things crop up all of the time."

He stared at her for a moment. "Can I ask you a personal question?"

After a moment's consideration, she nodded. "As long as I can choose whether I answer or not."

"Of course." He took a minute to frame his words with care. "I know you don't like the night. That's no big deal. But are you okay being alone with me, here, at night?"

She blushed, then nodded. "Yes. And if that changes, I'll let you know."

"Fair enough. I just wondered if you wanted to watch some television and have a beer? It's been a long day."

"Sure." She headed for the kitchen, opening the refrigerator. Grabbing two bottles, she handed one to him, then stopped to fill her favorite pottery bowl full of potato chips. "Take a seat. I'm going to call the boys." The dogs responded to her whistle, came over to be patted, and then settled on their beds in the corner. "How about a comedy?"

"Sounds good. We could use a laugh." They watched one, then another. Around eleven thirty, she had quieted, and he saw she'd fallen asleep. He didn't want to move, scared he would wake her.

Angus wanted to protect her. That might be crazy, because she could clearly take care of herself. The instinct persisted, nonetheless. He felt drawn to her, this smart, independent woman who was scared of the dark. *Such a contradiction.*

Unsure if Max would be mad when she woke, angry to find him still here, he chose to risk it so she could get some well-earned sleep. And maybe, in time, she would learn to associate his presence with calm and rest. Other men might mistake drama for passion, but for him, pleasure could often be a slow and sneaky thing. He wanted a combination of a best friend and lover. That would be worth the wait if he ever found it. Slouching down against the cushion, he closed his eyes.

****

*What the hell.* The watcher paced under the leafy cover of the spreading trees, trying to keep his brewing temper in check. Angus hadn't left her house. No one spent time with her at night, no one but him. That sonofabitch continued to steal their time together. He had no right.

Everyone kissed up to this lame guy, but he considered him no big deal. What—he writes a few dreary, academic books that nobody could even understand, and that makes him better than everyone else? It astonished him that a smart woman like Max would waste an hour on this nerd. No matter what, Dr. Big Deal couldn't just drop out of nowhere and steal his girl away. She'd always been special, special in a way only he truly understood.

Egghead better damn well leave the house soon, leave before he charged in after him to slice him to pieces. He watched, wallowing in pain for hours, before storming off into the night.

## Chapter Eleven

One of the dogs sniffing her fingers woke her the next morning. Still half-asleep, she drew her hand back, mumbling at him, before she stretched her legs. Her eyes shot open as her feet hit Angus's thigh.

She had a baffled moment before recalling them watching movies the previous night. Her brain played catch up as he opened his eyes, rubbing a hand over his face. "I guess we fell asleep."

"I guess so." Letting the dogs out to relieve themselves allowed her a moment to process her disbelief. She glanced at her watch. It read almost seven a.m. She had slept for an unheard of eight hours straight, something she hadn't been able to do for decades. She laughed, and even to her ears it sounded stilted.

"Did I miss something?" he asked, stretching.

Shrugging, she walked over to switch on the coffeemaker. "I just haven't slept so well in a long time, that's all."

"Must have been overdue," he replied. "If I can steal a cup of coffee to take with me, I'll get out of your hair so you can start your day."

A few minutes later, she watched as he sauntered down the hill to the trailer. She had a long, hot shower, taking plenty of time to wash her hair, then finished with a blast of cold to get herself moving. She got dressed, reminding herself that her dirty laundry needed to be done soon. After gathering the paint samples under her arm, she whistled for the dogs and headed to the site.

Nate showed up after the men started their work for the day, looking better than he had in a while. "You must be in a good mood this morning," she said, giving him a hug.

He nodded. "Last night, Emma told me the kids at school were asking questions about her mother."

"Oh, no. Was she upset?"

"Strangely, not at all, which surprised me. She told them she doesn't need a mommy, because she has a daddy, a Max, and an Agnus." He paused. "Don't you think it's strange how much she likes Angus?"

"Oh, I don't know. He's a very easy guy to have around."

"Hmmm." Nate cleared his throat. "I saw him leaving your place this morning."

She stopped peering at the plans, and, looking up, chuckled at his wary expression. "You should see your face, Nate. It's red all the way up to your ears."

"Is not."

"Is too." She sighed. "We just fell asleep watching television."

"You fell asleep or he did?"

"Both." She read his look of surprise. "I know. It kind of surprised me, too. I'll have to thank him for the extra energy. I haven't had that much sleep in years."

****

That evening, Angus was picking at his salad without much interest when someone interrupted by rapping on his door. He opened it to find Nate standing outside and invited him in. "Hope I'm not interrupting."

"Of course not." He waved at his plate. "I have more in the refrigerator if you want some."

Nate stared down at the salad, frowning. "No, thanks. I probably should, but truth is, I'm not much one for salads. It's more of a punishment than a meal."

Reaching into the crowded refrigerator, Angus grabbed him a beer instead, which he accepted, popping the top. "Everything okay?" Angus asked.

Nate nodded, taking a swig. "I want to ask you about something, man to man, if that's okay."

Talk about piquing his interest. "Of course. Go ahead."

"Are you interested in Max?"

Angus met the other man's gaze, noting the concern in his expression. "Yes. Is that a problem for you?" He took his seat and waved Nate to the opposite one.

The other man sighed as he sat. "Not a problem, exactly. More like a concern."

"Fair enough," Angus replied. "What exactly is your concern?"

Nate twisted his hands and finally settled them on his knees. "She's a great person, but she has baggage, you know. Baggage that can be hard for most people to understand."

"Everyone has baggage, Nate. Me included."

"I get your point. We're not kids, after all." He shifted in his seat. "I guess I just mean that, if you are interested, you better be seriously interested and not just playing around." His resting hand twitched.

Angus smothered a smile, touched at the other man's concern. He nodded. "I understand. I respect how you look out for her. Maybe it would help if you understand what my intentions are."

"Okay."

"At this point in my life, I'm looking for a partner, someone who will stay for the long run. I've had my share of superficial relationships, but now, I'm old enough to know what I want. Whether that could be Max or not remains to be seen." When Nate didn't say anything, he continued. "I plan to proceed slowly, so she doesn't feel put on the spot. Does my explanation help ease your concerns?"

Nate nodded, leaning forward. "Can I assume your baggage doesn't include a prolonged stay in jail or any kind of abuse?"

Angus met the other man's gaze, realizing that, with his background, he had every reason to be worried. "That's a safe assumption on your part."

"I'm not talking about a one-night bender when you raise a little hell that doesn't hurt anybody but you. I've had a few of those myself. I'm talking about if you're an abusive freak and I'll have to bury you in the back field somewhere."

Since he could visualize Nate doing exactly that to protect Max, he clarified. "My mother would have neutered me on the spot if I showed any such tendencies. Believe me, no jailer could be half as scary."

Nate leaned back, relaxing. "I hope I'm not stepping out of line by asking you about this."

"Not at all." He always appreciated a direct approach to anything. "I'm a pretty straight-forward person myself, so I appreciate your honesty."

Nate took another drink and swallowed. "You'll need patience."

"I'm a pretty patient guy. If it works out, it will be worth it."

Long after Nate left, Angus thought about his visit as he packed a suitcase for Louisville. He admired Nate and Max's connection. Having had no siblings, he had nothing to compare it to, but he'd often wondered what it would be like to have a brother or sister who would always leap to your defense.

Around ten, he went outside to pick up a few things he'd left on the table. The clear night sky boasted a host of stars, and he stopped to admire them. Suddenly, a streak of gray caught his peripheral vision. In the far end of the pasture, he could see Ghost trotting, shaking his head up and down. Curious, he moved to peer over the fence. *What got into him?*

Something shifted amongst the trees, and he blinked, trying to focus. When he looked again, it had disappeared. He clucked to Ghost, and he trotted over, mumbling in a deep tone, obviously out of sorts. "What's up, buddy?" Reaching up, he patted his head, and the horse blew through his nostrils, looking back. *A wild animal, I guess.*

When he settled down again, he wished him goodnight and went inside to bed.

The next morning, his flight to Louisville proved uneventful. By evening, he sat across from his mother at her favorite dinner club, pausing now and then to say hello to other patrons. It hadn't changed in decades, still boasting the oversized chandeliers and the scurrying wait staff dressed in black.

"Is the house almost finished?" Lina asked, sipping her martini.

"We're getting there," he answered. "I picked the paint colors before I left, so the painters will start work on that tomorrow."

"How exciting." She tilted her head. "And how is Max?"

"Busy as ever," he answered, ignoring the question in her eyes. "She just signed a contract on the house they'll work on after mine."

"I really enjoyed her." His mother's eyes sparkled. "She's feisty."

He laughed. "She has to be pretty feisty to work in a world dominated by men."

"Independent women make the best wives. I should know."

He sipped his drink. "That's a little obvious, Mother, even for you."

She tried, and failed, to conjure up an innocent look. "It might be rather fun to have grandchildren."

He began to answer, pausing when he noticed an ex-girlfriend making her way across the crowded dining room. Lina followed his gaze and hid a grin. "Here comes trouble," she whispered.

Carrie Wentworth, dressed in a form-fitting cocktail dress, leaned down to kiss Lina's cheek, then repeated the gesture with Angus. "Well, aren't the two of you a sight for sore eyes."

"Hello, Carrie," Lina replied. "I haven't seen you in a while. What have you and your father been up to?"

The slender blonde ran a manicured hand down one hip. “We just got back from Italy. Poor Daddy’s exhausted.”

“How is your father?”

She rolled her ice blue eyes, dramatic to the end. “He’s talking about retiring for the hundredth time. It’ll never happen, of course. He won’t survive without his endless chain of lackeys.” Turning her head, she switched her attention to Angus. “I heard you’re busy causing all kinds of drama, living like a hippy on a farm or some such thing.”

Her relentless snobbery grated on him. “Not everyone who has a home in the country lives on a farm, Carrie.”

Looking down her nose, she said, “Call it what you will, it’s hardly a penthouse, darling.”

He decided to needle her just a bit. “Actually, right now, I’m living in a motor home while my house is being renovated.”

“That’s taking shock value a little too far.” She offered a familiar pout, probably convinced it made her look sexy.

“It’s actually very peaceful,” he replied, baffled about what he’d ever seen in this woman.

“Peaceful is for monks,” she sneered. She blathered on, gossiping, and he had a hard time pretending to listen. After a moment, she waved her hand in a dismissive gesture and wandered off.

“I’m not sure what you ever saw in her,” his mother commented.

He chuckled. “I was just thinking the same thing. Hopefully, my taste has evolved.”

They enjoyed their delicious seafood dinner, sampling lobster and crab, but left shortly after, too full to consider dessert. Angus stopped at his mother's place for a nightcap. He looked around the elegant house he'd grown up in, with its gleaming antiques and sculptures. The beautiful décor was at his mother's instigation. His father could have cared less. Work had always been the only thing that appeared to engage him.

"Are you still happy living here?"

She paused to consider. "Happy enough, I guess. It's what I'm used to. You should have stayed here with me while you're in town."

"Too many late-night events and early morning meetings to drive back and forth in a rush." He turned to face her. "Do you ever feel lonely?" He wondered, too late, if his blunt question offended her, because she looked away for a moment.

"A little lonely, at times." She took a seat on her favorite floral sofa while he poured their drinks. "I still miss your father after all these years. I even miss his endless ranting about his business dealings. Isn't that peculiar?"

"Not at all." He handed her a liqueur and poured scotch for himself. "Have you ever thought about dating again?"

She raised her eyebrows. "Oh, I couldn't. I simply don't have the inclination to deal with someone else's needs anymore. All the men my age want either a nursemaid or a housekeeper. Not exactly my cup of tea."

"You could always find a younger man to chase you around the house."

"They'd just mess up my hair and try to steal my money. No, thank you."

He smiled at the thought. "Well, then, given your preferences, I want you to promise me one thing."

"All right."

"Any time you feel lonely, call to make sure I'm around, then just jump in the car and come visit me. You can stay as long as you like."

It startled him to see his mother brush a tear from the corner of her eye. "You're such a wonderful son, Angus. You really are."

Darn it, Max had been right. His mother was lonely. He would have to thank his neighbor later for pointing it out.

****

Max wandered around Angus's house, inspecting the newly painted rooms. She marked some areas requiring touchups which always happened, but the overall quality of the work pleased her. Construction would be finished within ten days, and, in part, she would regret seeing it come to a close. This had been her favorite house to work on thus far.

The property seemed too quiet to her, almost boring without Angus around. With any luck, in a day or two he'd be back. She looked forward to seeing him. Even Nate had become used to having him around, and he could be a hard sell when it came to making friends.

Whistling for the dogs, Max headed up the hill to her house. When she withdrew the keys from her pocket, she realized the front door cracked ajar a few inches. She opened it wider. "Nate? Are you here?"

She heard no response. Peeking in, she tried to decide whether or not to enter. Everything she could see from this standpoint appeared to be exactly the way she'd left it. Weighing the chances of an actual intruder, she paused. As she debated, Nate's pickup truck pulled into the driveway and he exited, Emma jumping out behind him. They called hello, their feet making crunching sounds as they crossed the gravel. "Everything okay?"

Her worries embarrassed her. "The front door was open. I couldn't decide if I should go in."

"Stay by the truck with Emma."

"Nate—"

"It's probably nothing, but let's be sure." Disappearing inside, he was gone for a bit and emerged several minutes later. "Everything's fine," he announced, patting her on the shoulder. He stopped and checked the lock. "Maybe you didn't quite shut it this morning and the wind caught it."

"I guess so. I've been a little distracted." She'd always been so careful, though. "As long as everything's okay."

Waiting until they drove down the driveway past her house, she went inside.

Max thought about her lapse later that night, chastising herself. She'd been so busy and would have to take more care with security. They didn't have many problems out here in the country, but, still, it paid to be cautious. Especially since she lived alone.

The next day, Max seriously considered going home to bed and pulling the covers up over her head to shield her from the mishaps of the day. Just after they got started working, the long-awaited granite counters showed up with not one, but two major flaws. The delivery crew, who she had never dealt with before, told her they weren't too bad. Surely, she could make do.

Twelve thousand dollars in granite, and they wanted her to make do. First, she tried tact, then she let them have it, both barrels. Construction gods didn't smile on weaklings.

After a lot of back and forth on the phone, she finally landed their boss's assurance they would recut her order, but it would still mean a few days' delay. She had planned for it to be a nice welcome home surprise for Angus. *Oh, well.*

After such disappointing news, her day continued to slide downhill. The building inspector found a small plumbing mistake in one of the bathrooms. Just her luck, the plumber had the flu and couldn't come back to fix the issue for a few more days. She sat for a moment, trying to figure out what could possibly get done that day so the time wouldn't be a total waste.

As she sat grumbling to herself, she received a text from Angus, saying his return home would be delayed two more days. Apparently, his problems with the research study were more complicated than originally thought. She swallowed a shriek of frustration. *Problems seem to come in threes, so let's hope that's it for this week.*

When Nate showed up to see the counters, she unloaded her frustrations on him, the vexing issues spewing out like a gush from a broken faucet. He gave her a hug. "I know you, and what you need is some sleep."

"Don't be a jackass. It's not even noon." She scrubbed at her face, knowing she was cranky, which bugged her even more.

"Did you get any sleep at all last night?"

She sighed. "I just couldn't believe I left the damn door open."

He ruffled her hair. "I'll keep an eye on things and putter. You need to catch some zees." Meeting her gaze, he pointed in the direction of her place. "After I pick up Em from school, the three of us can grab burgers and shakes for an early dinner."

"We eat way too many burgers and shakes, you know. I should have a salad instead."

"Save the salad for tomorrow. You need happy grub today."

"Okay." Leaning over, she kissed his cheek and left, wondering what she would ever do without him. At home, she turned on the television and promptly fell asleep for almost four hours. When she woke, she felt more like herself.

****

He'd almost been caught inside her house, warned only by the sound of her truck wheels on the driveway. The spearing jolt of adrenaline as he slipped through the back door with only seconds to spare gave him an unexpected thrill. His heart pounded as he ran, skirting the property line, using the trees to shelter him.

Taking a moment to stuff one of her T-shirts from the laundry basket inside his jacket had cost him a precious minute. Well worth the risk, he thought, as he stroked it against his stubbled cheek, inhaling her scent.

It had been a much happier week with the dweeb out of town. Almost being caught in the pasture before he left had given him a moment of concern, but, ultimately, he hadn't really seen anything. And it's not like the damn horse could talk, even if he'd made a fuss, charging around the field.

He'd found the opportunity to steal into Max's house twice this week, trailing his fingers everywhere she touched. Investigating her bedroom offered the best rewards. Lying on her bed, visualizing her beneath him, had almost paralyzed him before he forced himself to move on. On the way out, unable to resist, he'd shoved a pair of lace panties from her lingerie drawer into his pocket.

Searching through the precious photograph albums he'd found in the armoire had yielded a photograph from the year they'd met. He'd stared at it, so ecstatic it made his hands tremble, then slid it from the plastic envelope into his wallet. She'd never miss it. She probably hadn't looked at those photos in years.

He considered it his prize possession, a trophy of sorts, his reward for being so unbelievably patient until the right time arrived. Now, every night, before bed, he could stare at that picture as he fell asleep to dream of her. And, before too long, the picture would be replaced by the real thing.

And no one could say it was inappropriate anymore.

## Chapter Twelve

Angus did some basic exercises in his hotel suite, rolling his shoulders in a failed attempt to relax. There were always territorial issues involved in academic life, but it irritated him when someone let their ego complicate a job. A solution-oriented person, he concentrated on making the various steps of an experiment work, rather than worrying about gathering acclaim at every step.

The scientist in charge of this study complicated the process by slowing the work down, intimidated by another person taking over his project. He seemed a little resentful Angus had figured out the solution. Despite being a patient man, it frustrated him.

He longed to go home. Not that he didn't enjoy the beautiful city of Louisville, but it couldn't compare to his wonderful new house. As he pulled off his clothes to prepare for bed, he promised himself to concentrate on work-from-home jobs in the future. He had discovered that he stayed much more productive there, thanks to the peace and quiet. And the boundless virtues of having no commute, ever again, enticed him.

They were a mere two weeks away from the expected completion date on his house at this point. He couldn't wait to see the progress they'd made while he took care of this job and hoped there would be no delays.

Upon completion, he would throw a festive party with the construction crew and Ian there to celebrate. His mother could come for the weekend and meet everyone.

He counted on the new furniture arriving as scheduled or no one would have anywhere to sit. Max would help him decide on the right setup for dancing, tables, and chairs. Nate had started on his dining table, and he picked everything else to accent it as he considered his friend's creation a work of art.

Just trying to visualize the end result helped him fall asleep.

****

Despite the extra rest, Max woke up the following day feeling jittery. She had checked the door three times last night, a little obsessive even for her. Her laundry basket had disappeared only to reappear in her spare room. A creature of habit, she always left it either on the washer or in the bathroom corner. *What's wrong with me?*

Max could hear her father's voice echo in her ears as if to answer the unspoken question. *No man will ever want you, Adrienne. You're not that smart, and there isn't a feminine bone in your body.* Shaking the ugly words away, she climbed into the shower. No wonder she had grown to hate her given name.

Although she hadn't seen her father for years before his death, sometimes his abusive words still echoed in her memory. Even after all of these years, when she was off her game, his denigrating comments were what filled her mind. She would have had no self-esteem at all as a young person if it weren't for her mother's healthy influence and Nate's constant support.

Turning on the spray, she let warm water stream down her face. She picked up her bar of soap and scrubbed, only gentling when her skin began to sting. Chill out, she told herself. She wasn't alone, not by a long shot. She had Nate, Emma, and Angus.

*Angus?*

Stopping, mid-motion, she gasped as water trickled into her mouth, making her choke. She coughed, then took a deep breath to calm her lungs down. Including Angus had happened spontaneously, and that was both troubling and scary. She couldn't afford to include Angus.

Her parents provided a terrific example of why people shouldn't get married. Besides that, her phobia meant marriage had always been off the cards for her. The kind of men she liked were the marrying kind, but she wasn't. That had discouraged her from dating for years.

She'd also realized at some point in the last decade that putting up with the shenanigans most women did wouldn't work for her, either. Cheaters or abusers should end up with their parts removed by a rusty knife. And men who thought women should be thrilled to scrub their underwear and stay chained to the kitchen would always be encouraged to exit, stage left.

Who did that leave, she wondered? Only that rarest of creatures: a decent, smart guy who thought a woman scared of the dark would be the ultimate prize. *Give me a break.*

Finishing her shower, she toweled off. She glanced in the mirror and realized she needed a haircut. When she had free time, she'd schedule it. That might not be anytime soon, the way things were going.

As she dressed, she made a plan to keep her mind occupied. Going to the hardware store and picking up the towel racks she had ordered would allow fresh air to clear her mind and set her up for a more productive day.

Late in the afternoon, she started to feel more upbeat. Being proficient at her job always boosted her confidence. She installed the towel bars and toilet paper holders, waving Pete away when he offered to help. Sometimes the man just hovered too much, and it could be a little annoying at times.

Nate had returned, and he stayed busy installing the first of the large built-ins with Emma's dubious assistance. The house was really starting to come together. She couldn't wait to see Angus's reaction.

Pete installed the locks and deadbolts on all of the outside doors. No point in tempting any wandering burglars, although they didn't have many problems this far out in the country. Last year, Ian had caught a man trying to walk away from a competitor's project with a brand-new HVAC air conditioning unit worth six thousand dollars. It paid to be proactive.

After they completed the day's work, Max helped Emma with her homework while Nate fixed their leaky toilet. She walked home as the day neared sunset, stopping to give Ghost his goodnight scratch on the head. Thumbing through the mail she picked out of the postbox, she entered the kitchen, trying to figure out what would be the easiest dish to make for supper.

The scent of tomato sauce stopped her in her tracks. Following it to the sink, she spied a dirty dish waiting there with silverware. She stared at it as if it were an alien. She hadn't put it there. Last night, dinner had been burgers with Nate and Emma.

She hadn't slept well. *Is it possible to eat a snack you don't remember?*

Maybe her lack of sleep was catching up with her. Could she be sleepwalking? After all, nobody else had been in the house.

*Had they?*

Of, course, they hadn't. To reassure herself, she walked through all of the rooms, opening the closets and checking under the bed even though it made her feel foolish. Nothing seemed to be missing or been tampered with as far as she could tell. The dogs trailed after her, stopping and sniffing, as if this was a new game.

After her exercise in paranoia, Max put it out of her mind or at least tried. She threw together a sandwich with some fruit for dessert and settled down in front of the television.

****

He had copied her house keys last year, when she'd left them on the work bench one day in a rare moment of forgetfulness. A quick trip into town had taken care of that chore. Too busy to notice, she never even realized they'd been missing.

Never really intending to use them, he now realized the time had come to show her that she needed him for protection. Small discrepancies around the house should worry her, like a door left open or a dirty plate she didn't remember. He wondered how she'd reacted when she found the food-stained dishes. *A little paranoid? Good.* She needed to understand that a strong man like him could keep her safe from herself.

If it weren't for those damn dogs, he would creep in during the night and watch her as she slept. They didn't really care for him. Animals never did. So, the only time he could enter was when they were outside. He tried to content himself with loving her from afar, but now his territory was being challenged.

He needed to step up his game.

Concern about her phone messages distracted him. That idiot Alan Patterson had been bothering her again. He was a preening peacock, a loser who let Daddy pay his bills. The few times they had run into each other, the jerk called him short stuff. An idiot like him wasn't fit to be in the same room as his beloved.

And how would Max feel if she knew the lawyer's secret? Mr. Hot Stuff paid a hooker to bounce on him once a week like clockwork. He grinned at the knowledge, and it suddenly gave birth to an irresistible idea.

Patterson was in for the ride of his life.

****

Angus caught the first flight of the day out of the bustling Louisville International Airport, grateful for no further delays. He enjoyed the anticipation of seeing his home and wondering what had been added in his absence. Seeing Max would be a bonus.

He found nobody on site when he arrived. *Silly to feel disappointed.* As he wandered through, looking for the missing countertops, Max showed up and explained why they weren't installed. "The paint looks great, though," he said, smiling.

"Good. Come and look at the bathrooms."

Surprised to see them finished, he said, "So, let's see. We're down to countertops in the kitchen, light fixtures, and landscaping?"

Max nodded, smiling. “And Nate finished your table last night. It’s stunning. Thank goodness for your sliding doors. That might be the only way we can get the table inside.”

“You guys are amazing.”

She bowed. “Thank you. Although the counters were delayed, we managed to arrange your furniture delivery for the day after tomorrow. The company we use owed me a favor.”

He sighed. “This is the best welcome home ever.”

“You look a little tired. Was your job frustrating?”

Nodding, he leaned against the wall. “Apparently, I stepped on another man’s toes, just by showing up to help. It made for long days with unnecessary stress.”

“Well, that’s frustrating. How’s your mom?”

“Good.” He met her gaze. “I owe you one, though.”

“Oh? Why?”

“You were right about her being lonely. I should have caught it and I didn’t.”

She patted his arm. “You’re a man. Not your strong point.”

“Ouch,” he joked. “A little sexist, but probably well-deserved.”

“Did you suggest anything that might help?”

“Well, apparently, she doesn’t want to date again.” He shrugged. “She’s pretty clear about that.”

“I’m proud you could stand the idea. A lot of grown children can’t.”

He nodded. “I told her if she gets lonely, she should just hop in the car and come, any time she likes.”

Max raised her eyebrows. "I bet most parents never get such an open invitation. Good for you."

"How about your mother?"

She glanced away. "My mother died when I was ten."

"I'm sorry. What about your father?"

Restless, she began to wander. "My father and I weren't close. He died a few years ago."

"An obvious sore spot. I apologize for asking."

Looking surprised, she met his gaze. "It's not a problem. That's why I call Nate and Emma my family."

"I don't blame you. Where are they, by the way? They're usually hanging around by now."

"Since Emma had a day off from school for teacher training, he took her to the movies. They wanted to have fun before his dreaded responsibilities tonight."

"And what's that?"

"Parent teacher night at school."

"Oh, fun."

She laughed. "Not his favorite thing. You know why?"

Angus shook his head.

"Emma's teacher has a crush on him and rubs his arm all night long. It drives him crazy."

"In a good way?"

Max slapped a hand over her mouth to corral a louder laugh and spoke through her spread fingers. "She's sixty if she's a day. It's a little creepy, to be honest."

"Interesting. I never think of women as being creepy, but I guess there might be exceptions to the rule." He watched as she walked around to check doors and windows, locking up the place. "Why don't we sit and have a cold beer? Afterward, I'll make you the best soup and salad combo you've ever had."

"At my place?"

"Sure, if you'd prefer."

"That sounds great. Give me ten minutes to tidy up and we'll be all set."

****

The evening began much as movie night had with him preparing the food and her hanging over the counter to chat. At some point, she paused to listen to her messages on speaker, sighing when she listened to the last one; Alan Patterson, asking her out to dinner.

"He doesn't exactly take the hint, does he?" Angus tossed the salad and set it aside.

She groaned and shook her head. "To tell you the truth, I'm not sure what his problem is."

"Maybe he's never heard the word 'no.' "

"Oh, I'm pretty sure he's heard it from lots of women, but maybe just can't believe it." She laughed. "I guess I just don't understand people like that. Why would you bother to waste time pursuing someone who's clearly not interested?"

"Exactly. One good kick to the ego is usually enough." He sliced their sandwiches in half. "Do you ever call him back?"

"No, not after the second time."

He raised his eyebrows. "How many times has he asked?"

"This is number ten. I keep count out of sheer disbelief."

"Good lord. Your devoted admirer needs to find another pastime." He put a sandwich and some salad on each plate, handing her one. Following her to the couch with his own, he sat while she moved their drinks to the coffee table.

"It's become worse since he bumped into us together at the farmer's market." *Now, why the hell did I let that slip?*

"Really," Angus replied. "That's interesting. So, he can deal with rejection as long as he's sure you have no one else at your beck and call."

She shoved a big bite of sandwich in her mouth to give her a minute to consider how to respond. The tart taste of cranberry surprised her. "This is delicious. What did you add to the turkey?"

"Cranberry and blue cheese with a few herbs. Do you like it?"

"It's amazing." Max realized, after a moment, she was making a purring sound of enjoyment as she ate. "Sorry."

He laughed. "Best compliment ever."

They ate the rest of the meal in silence. Afterward, she carried the dishes out and fetched them both a second beer. "I'd suggest having you pay off your house in meal exchanges, but I'm worried Nate and I would die of obesity."

He nodded. "I try to eat salads fifty percent of the time as penance for the other stuff, but the operative word is 'try.' And since I'm now apparently addicted to Bo's shakes and burgers, I need to try even harder."

"That's fair." She settled back on the opposite end of the couch. "I can't believe how fast the last two months have gone by. Are you excited about your house almost being finished?"

Angus nodded. "I'm rather surprised how much I'm looking forward to it. I really missed watching all of the progress while I worked in Louisville." He met her gaze. "I want to have a party for the crew and everyone after it's done."

"That's a great idea. They'll enjoy that."

"I thought I'd cook a ton of pasta, and we'll buy beer and wine. Maybe find some desserts and bread to round things out."

"Perfect."

"If you could hand pick the perfect life partner for yourself, what qualities would he have to possess?"

The change of subjects gave her whiplash. "W-what?"

"You heard me." Leaning back to give her space, he smiled.

Returning to the discussion about food would have been easier. She sighed. "My phobia kind of makes that a complicated issue."

"Forget about your phobia for the moment and answer the question, just as a theoretical exercise."

Nerves tightened her throat. "I guess smart and funny are at the top of the list."

"Me, too." He encouraged her with one hand. "What else?"

"Loyal. Monogamous."

He cocked his head. "So, you wouldn't put up with a cheater?"

"Nope. Not abusers, either. They're both a call for a rusty knife neuter as far as I'm concerned."

"I agree," he replied. "Although that's a rather dramatic way to put it." He patted the cushion beside him.

She moved closer before she identified the emotion that compelled her to do it. “Why are you asking me all these questions?”

“You’re a smart lady. You already know the answer to that.” He waited, just watching, and because he didn’t rush her, she sidled near him so their legs touched.

“Angus…”

He kissed her then, one hand on either side of her face, taking his time. She was the one who pushed closer, her arms slipping down his back and pulling him tight. His body felt so good to her, all firm muscles and man. She ran her hands up to comb through his hair and back down again, then suddenly found herself stretched out beside him.

Every time they progressed, he let her choose the next step. It made her feel a power in her own body she’d never experienced. When she began to unbutton his shirt, he whispered, “Are you sure, Max?”

Trembling, she answered, “Yes.”

Without another word, he paused. He pushed her hands away long enough to stand and lift her as if she weighed ounces. With long strides, he crossed the den, nudging her bedroom door open with his foot. He lay her on the bed with great care. She watched as he stripped off his clothes, then helped her with hers.

Just looking at him naked revved her senses, making a mockery of his nerd designation. His broad shoulders framed his chest and tapered to, oh my, everything else below. She reached one hand up, imploring, and he rejoined her, emanating heat and energy. Raising up, she touched him everywhere, watching him grit his teeth in pleasure. It spurred her on in her quest to discover what lay beyond his control. After a few more minutes of exploration, he lowered to let his body graze hers, letting her embrace that first real shock of connection.

His teeth closing gently on her neck made her utter a sound she'd never made before, one of yearning. Instinct drove him to all the right places, his hands and his mouth driving her until she couldn't bear it. She could feel him, ready and waiting, and whispered, "Please."

He eased inside her, inch by precious inch, until she grasped him from within. They started to move, and she became the impatient one, writhing and squirming for the best contact. The boom of her heart against his filled her senses, like a beating drum in some ancient mating ritual.

Dragging her nails down his back made him groan. His rhythm increased as she said his name, and he murmured hers in response. Feeling wrapped up in him, she came, long and gasping, tightening as he joined her a moment later.

Panting, they stayed together while their hearts slowed. He pulled her to lay on top of him, running a hand down her back. After a minute, he spoke. "Words fail me right now." When she didn't respond, he used a finger to lift her face and stare into her eyes. "Are you okay? I didn't hurt you, did I?"

She smiled. "If pain gave that result, I might volunteer." Running a hand over his bicep, she asked, "Do you think studying the human body makes you better at this kind of thing?"

"I've never thought about it." He folded one arm under his head. "I don't have any alternative experience to use as a comparison."

"That's my version of a compliment."

"I took it as such. If I thought my legs would hold me, I'd give a humble bow."

She popped him on the arm. "Turkey." Gazing into his eyes, she saw a slumbering pleasure tinged with humor. "Are you going to stay?"

"Unless you ask me to leave."

Shaking her head, she moved back and slipped into the crook of his arm. After a few minutes, she said, "This is complicated."

One hand stroked her hair. "Save the introspection for tomorrow," he suggested.

An inborn sense of priorities insisted she agree.

## Chapter Thirteen

She woke the next morning to a sense of confusion before remembering with pleasure the events of the preceding night. Stretching her limbs every which way, she became hungry as she recognized the smell of bacon. Angus's voice murmured in the distance, and she realized he was talking to the dogs.

Grabbing a quick shower, she dressed, then entered the kitchen. "Good morning," she said, trying not to feel awkward. "You're going to an awful lot of trouble. I don't usually eat much for breakfast."

"That's sacrilegious. Breakfast is the most important meal of the day." Angus turned away from the pan and took a step closer to drop a kiss on her cheek. "I let the dogs out for a few minutes, but I wasn't sure what you feed them and how much."

She laughed at their plaintive expressions and went over to a cupboard, reaching in to scoop food into their bowls. Three tails whipped with enthusiasm as she rationed it. As she turned back, Angus dished out eggs and bacon, adding buttered toast he had apparently left warming in the oven. He handed her a plate. "Dig in while it's hot."

"You're kind of bossy in the morning, you know." She took a bite of toast, realizing she really did feel hungry.

"Guilty as charged." He smiled. "And not just in the morning, either." Chewing, he strolled to the refrigerator and peered inside. "Want a glass of milk?"

"No, I'm good for now."

He poured himself a glass and drank it down.

The sight of it made her giggle. "So, you like milk, I guess."

"How do you think I grew this tall?" He strolled back and finished off his eggs. "My mother used to say we should keep a cow or two in the pantry, just for me, instead of needing half of the refrigerator space for milk."

"What kind of kid were you?"

He pushed away his empty plate. "The stereotypical nerd kid. I'll bet that surprises you."

"Really?"

He laughed, and the hearty sound of it made her smile. "Yes. Black-framed glasses, pocket protector and all. And I was so skinny and tall my mother had to have jeans tailored for me because nothing off the rack fit."

"You probably drove all the brainy girls wild."

He shrugged. "Afraid not. Besides, girls were scarier than poisonous snakes in those days."

"So, when did that change? High school?"

"No. High school was hell on steroids. I made a habit of getting bullied by the jocks, which persuaded me to work extra hard and graduate a year early just to escape."

A wave of sympathy for the child he'd been touched her heart. "Yeah. Nate and I didn't have much fun in high school, either."

He grinned. "I guess we're all much more successful at being adults."

"True. Thank goodness for that." She watched as he slid the dirty dishes into the dishwasher. "Thanks."

"No problem." He washed his hands. "I'll check in a little later. I have a few calls to make and some paperwork to catch up on." He walked past her, sliding a hand over her hair and kissing her.

Max watched as he closed the door behind him. She'd expected to feel like an idiot, but it hadn't been awkward at all.

*Is that a good thing, or does it complicate things even more?*

****

Angus found himself whistling as he walked down the grassy hill toward his home on wheels, enjoying the heat of the morning sun. He'd handled that rather well, he thought, giving himself a figural pat on the back.

Knowing Max would feel off balance with him in the house this morning, he'd tried to keep things as normal as possible, concentrating on food and avoiding intimate conversation. He hadn't missed her expression of relief when he had.

But the memory of making love to her made him whistle. You couldn't possibly come up with a better way to start the day. He understood enough about women, though, to know giving her space to figure things out might be a smart idea.

And the question about their physical chemistry had been answered in capital letters.

Besides, he really did have some articles to review for a journal and a textbook proposal to write. He would try to get a lot of it done today, so he could watch the furniture being put in place tomorrow. Max had already promised to arrange it for him. He wouldn't know where to begin. He said good morning to Ghost who grazed by the fence as he entered his place, then got down to work.

Late in the afternoon, a frantic thumping sounded on his door before he jumped up and yanked it open. Max stood waiting, out of breath and looking disheveled. “We need you.”

“What’s wrong?” Hearing the urgency in her tone, he rushed, yanking on his shoes and throwing his reading glasses onto the table.

“Em came home with a really bad stomachache.”

“Where is she?”

She pointed at Nate’s truck, parked slanted across the path. He could see Nate’s silhouette in the driver’s seat and ran in that direction, leaning in the open passenger door. Em was lying in his lap, limp and pale. He smelled vomit and spied it on the rubber floormat. “Where does it hurt?”

Nate’s worried gaze met his as Emma sobbed. “Her stomach.”

“Show me where.”

Nate pointed to her lower right belly. “Should we call an ambulance?”

He shook his head, trying not to frighten them. “No. Let’s take her. Max, slide in beside Nate. I’ll come next to you, and she can lie on our laps and be strapped in.” They scrambled to do as he suggested. When they were belted, Nate threw the truck into gear and hit the gas, splattering gravel.

When they reached the pavement, he sped up, arrowing toward town. Max’s eyes met Angus’s and he read the fear there. “Do you know the phone number of the hospital?”

She pulled her cell phone out of her rear pocket and handed it to him. "It's number two on speed dial."

Angus tried to ignore the pull of concern as he waited for someone on the other end to pick up. He finally got connected with the emergency room. "This is Dr. McLaren speaking. I am on my way into town with a six-year-old female child with appendicitis, possibly a rupture. She is flushed, vomiting, and experiencing severe pain. We are—how far away, Nate?"

"Eight, nine minutes."

"Eight or nine minutes away. Please inform the staff this is urgent. Her name is Emma Marshall."

As he hung up, he realized Emma's cries had weakened to a trembling groan. He stroked the side of her pale cheek. "We're almost there, Em. Don't worry. You're going to be okay." He could only pray he was right, seeing sweat had dampened her hair. "Did she feel okay at school?"

"She vomited the first time while she was waiting for me to pick her up," Nate ground out, his eyes focused on the road. "They said she'd been fine until then." He took a deep breath. "I thought it must be the stomach flu that's been going around, but the pain became a lot worse by the time we got to Max's."

After they arrived within town limits, Nate blew through the first stop sign because no other cars waited at the intersection. He ran a late yellow to reach the street they needed to turn onto, and they heard a siren start up behind them. They ignored it, gunning down the street to the hospital, cornering into the emergency room lane. After they yanked to a stop, the sliding glass doors opened, and two uniformed figures hustled out with a stretcher.

"Is this Emma?" the young woman closest to them asked.

"Yes," Nate answered. They scrambled to free her from the seatbelts. Nate scooped his daughter gently into his arms, transferring her to the gurney.

A deputy had climbed out of the car following them and watched the action as Nate and Max followed. The nurses trundled her inside the building. Angus stopped to explain, but the deputy waved him on. "Go on. I get it. No problem."

They followed the gurney down a long hall lit by glaring lights until they were stopped by a charge nurse. "Who's her father?" she asked, her hands on her hips.

"I am," Nate answered.

She gestured for him to follow. "Dad, you can come with us. The rest of you go back to the visitor's lounge and wait there." They disappeared down another hallway.

Angus stood with Max, frozen with worry for a moment. She turned, and he put his arms around her to comfort both of them. Her voice muffled, she asked, "Is she going to be okay?"

"I think so. We got her here quickly."

"Are you sure it's her appendix?"

He nodded. "Those are pretty specific symptoms. I'd be shocked if it turned out to be anything else."

"What will they do to her?" She pulled away to look up at his face.

Stroking her hair, he said, "They will likely have to remove it. I would expect her white cell count will be sky high at this point. They really have no other option."

"Poor Nate." She rubbed away her tears. "She's never been sick before."

"That's a good thing. It means she's healthy and she'll heal quickly." He said the words to reassure himself as much as her. It didn't take away the fear. Any operation, especially for a child already in pain, involved a certain level of risk.

Retreating thirty feet to the empty waiting room, they took seats on the hard, plastic chairs. Max stayed quiet for a while. Finally, she spoke. "I've never heard you use your title before."

"It has its uses."

She gave a faint smile. "You knew they would assume you're a medical doctor."

"I wanted to guarantee they took it seriously, and it worked. Every minute counts with an urgent case."

"Thanks for thinking of that."

He put his arm around her shoulders, and she laid her head on him. After another twenty minutes, Nate came through the swinging doors. They both sprang to their feet. "What's happening?" she asked.

"They gave her an injection to stop the vomiting. She's on her way to the operating room." He ran restless fingers through his hair and waved them back to their seats, joining them. "I know the doctor that's doing the surgery. Remember Dr. Cox?" Max nodded. "We worked on his house a few years ago. He said it will be at least an hour before they're finished and I can see her."

Angus stood. "I'll go to the cafeteria and get us all something to eat and drink."

"I can't eat anything until I know she's okay."

He met Nate's gaze. "She's going to be fine. We all need to be strong enough to take care of her, right?"

The other man gave a curt nod, and Angus turned to leave.

"Angus."

"Yes?"

"Thank you for saving my Emma's life."

He shrugged. "You would have found her the help she needed, regardless. Besides, I know you'd do the same for me, Nate." With relief lightening the tightness in his chest, he headed down to find something for them to eat.

On his return, they choked down about half of the food he bought, the best any of them could manage. The wait seemed interminable, and just when they could stand it no longer, the doctor came out to talk to them.

"She came through it like a champ and is resting comfortably. Nate, you can sit with her now. You two can have a short visit after she's awake and we move her to a regular bed." He glanced at his watch. "It was a rupture so it's a good thing you brought her to us as quickly as you did. She's a lucky girl." He patted Nate on the arm and pointed toward the recovery wing, asking a nurse to escort him.

Two hours later, a groggy Emma held court at her bedside. "They took my part and threw it away," she moaned, looking pale and rather indignant. "I wanted to keep it."

Max laughed. "Why?"

"To take to show and tell," she replied, as if everybody should know that.

After the laughter died down, she turned to Nate. "Why do I have to sleep here tonight, Daddy? They said a doctor needs to check me, but why can't Agnus check me?" A rare, whiny tone colored the words.

Angus stepped forward. "I'm not the right kind of doctor, Emma."

"It's okay with me," she replied.

He shook his head. "You need the doctor who operated to make sure you're okay. After that, you can come home and get spoiled for a while."

She paused. "Like ice cream spoiled?"

"Yes," answered Nate.

"And pretty gifts to open spoiled?"

Max smiled. "I think so, if you behave yourself. Right now, you have to get some sleep."

"Okay." Emma yawned. "But I'm not sleepy." In a few minutes, she had dozed off, nestled against her pillow in a halo of tangled hair.

The attentive nurse stepped in, pointing to her watch.

They got to their feet. "Angus and I need to go, Nate. I'll bring you guys fresh clothes in the morning. What else do you need?"

Nate glanced at his daughter. "I have everything I need right here."

## Chapter Fourteen

On the short drive home, he and Max stayed silent, recovering from the frantic pace and the fear. The parting image of Nate and Emma occupied his thoughts. All he could think about was that it represented everything he wanted in his life, a sense of connection and importance. Love didn't protect you from fear, but it certainly made it easier to bear.

"What are you thinking about?"

He glanced at her. "That some people truly understand the concept of family and some never do. It's rather ironic that she has both extremes with her parents."

"True." She sighed. "Just the thought of her being in pain makes me feel ill."

"Me, too."

"You didn't look it."

"That wouldn't be manly," he said, in an extra deep voice to make her laugh.

She chuckled, then sobered again. "I could tell it terrified Nate, but I didn't know what else I could say."

"You were there to support him. That's all he needed."

She straightened as they turned into her driveway. "Do you still have work to do? I know we interrupted you."

"There's nothing that can't wait until tomorrow. With all that draining adrenaline, my energy's gone."

"Why don't I make us both some dinner?"

He opened the door. "Compromise. Let me shower and change, then I'll come up and make dinner. Will that work?"

"That'd be great. I'll see you in a few minutes."

****

Pete sat in his truck, biding his time, his adrenaline already spiking. Alan Patterson was incredibly predictable, especially when it came to his weekly visit to his favorite whore. He chose this particular road because it was steep and narrow. There wasn't a lot of traffic. No one would see him heading down the track to Sammy Jo's trailer.

Or that was the theory.

Watching Patterson come and go the last two weeks had allowed him to form a plan. Third time's the charm, he thought with a self-satisfied grin. All he had to do was screech out in front of him, lights glaring, and watch the fun. The steep and rocky hillside created a long, steel bronco ride to the bottom.

He kept checking with his binoculars, and at ten fifteen he saw Alan's car winding up the opposite side of the hill. A thorough look both ways showed no one anywhere around. He counted the seconds off in his head. As he saw the car lights moving toward them, he shoved his gearshift into drive, keeping his foot pressed hard on the brake. He revved the engine.

As Alan approached the blind turn, Pete took his foot off the brake, and his truck blasted into the available space, sliding on the dirt. His bright lights blazed.

Reflexes made the other man yank his car away from the possibility of collision. He over-corrected, fish-tailed, then went sailing over the edge. There was a long, suspended pause before the horrendous crunch of metal on rock reverberated up the slope as the vehicle impacted somewhere in the trees far below.

Part of him hoped for a burst of flame to finish the job, but that didn't happen as often as people thought. Shoving his truck into park near the edge, he looked out of his window and down. Other than the drifting dust, there was no sign of the wreck from the road.

*Good.* That meant it would take a while for them to find him.

He rubbed his hands with glee, playing back the way the car had sailed over the edge in his mind. Putting his truck into gear, he started whistling as he drove toward home.

*Who's the short stuff now, loser?*

****

Max woke up the next morning in bed, fully dressed. After a minute, the disoriented feeling waned. She couldn't even remember climbing into bed, but Angus lay beside her, snoring. He must have carried her from the couch again.

Walking into the den, she let the dogs out and picked up her phone to text Nate. He answered immediately, saying Emma had slept all night and woken up hungry, a happy result expected by everyone.

Enjoying a lingering shower in the spare bathroom so as not to awaken Angus, she saw he still slept on her return. She walked back into the bedroom and tapped him on the arm. "Hey, sleepyhead."

His eyes flicked open as if powered by a switch, and she read the invitation in them.

"Good luck with that." She smiled. "It's almost eight, and the counters are supposed to arrive in thirty minutes."

He sighed. "Damn. I forgot."

"I thought you were excited about getting them."

He raised an eyebrow. "I can get excited about a lot of things."

"Very funny. Get your butt in gear. We're running behind."

She fed the dogs and, after his quick shower, the two of them settled on toast for a hasty breakfast. By the time they made their way down the hill, the landscapers were already hard at work, planting flowers and shrubs to add definition to the architecture of the house. He'd asked for low maintenance since he had no gardening skills, but he couldn't deny the additions gave the property a more finished look.

A few scant minutes after they arrived and unlocked the house, the tradesmen's truck rumbled down the driveway, someone at the wheel giving a cheery beep of the horn. The workers hefted the massive pieces of granite with great care up the front steps and into the kitchen. After they maneuvered them into place, they completed the finish work and departed, leaving the others to admire their work.

Angus had chosen a slab of granite with lots of pattern in the stone, brown and gold with a subtle touch of green. It made a dramatic centerpiece for the spacious kitchen with the newly installed copper lights as accents that shone from above.

"It's your favorite room, isn't it?" Max stood next to him, grinning, as he stared at his surroundings, transfixed.

"Absolutely."

"You look like a kid on Christmas morning."

He looped an arm around her and gave her a hug. "That's all thanks to you."

"And the guys, and your budget, and the construction gods smiling down on us."

"Fair enough."

She cocked her head, and, hearing another truck approaching, strolled to the front window to peer out. "Oh, my goodness. That's your furniture. I wasn't expecting them until this afternoon."

"Is everything ready?" He appeared nervous, a rarity for him.

"Yup. They'll place it wherever we want."

A manic whirlwind of activity filled the next two hours. Max stood beside the front entrance, list in hand, directing the three muscled delivery men like a traffic cop. He just kept out of the way out of respect for her system.

Once the workers unloaded everything into the proper rooms, they unwrapped each item from its protective layers. After that, she walked around and had them put each piece of furniture where it belonged. To add the final details, she moved the accessories into position herself.

When she came back downstairs, she found Angus wandering around, staring at each item and running his hand over it before moving on to the next.

"Feeling overwhelmed?" She had been through this process many times, but he hadn't.

"A little."

"Don't worry." Max smiled. "If you change your mind about anything, they'll swap it out for something else, as long as it isn't damaged in the meantime."

Angus shook his head. "I doubt I'll want to. It's just I'm comparing these things to what the decorator did in my old place. I can't believe how much more I like this. It's as if I'm getting the home and the life I never knew I wanted, all at once."

His words touched her. "Well, good. That's the point, isn't it?" She stopped to adjust a lamp shade. "What's your favorite piece?"

He paused to have a thorough look around. "Besides the table that's coming from Nate, the sofa, I guess. It's really hard to find one that's comfortable for a man of my height."

"Oh, my goodness." Max glanced at her watch. "In all the rush, I forgot about taking fresh clothes in to Nate." She headed toward the front door, then hesitated. "How busy are you this morning?"

"I've got some time available. What do you need?"

"The rest of the light fixtures are due to be delivered around lunch time. After the guys eat, they'll come and install them. Can you let them in? I'll bring you a late lunch on my way back."

"Of course. No problem."

She came back to give him a peck on the cheek. "You're the best."

Using her spare key to enter Nate's house, she dug around for some clean clothes and added Emma's favorite stuffed bear to the mix. A quick stop at the general store on her way to the hospital allowed her to purchase a book and a plastic horse as treats to keep Emma from becoming too bored.

As Max entered the hospital room, she heard Dr. Cox talking, so she stayed in the background. Nate looked relieved, but Emma whined, "I want to go home," her lip protruding.

"If you feel okey-dokey tomorrow morning, you can go home."

"I feel okey-dokey now."

The doctor patted her on the arm. "You need to try eating more food and go to the bathroom first."

"I already tinkled."

Nate tickled her chin. "Did ya poop?"

"I don't wanna poop." She crossed her arms.

Max moved forward. "They have to be sure your parts are working, silly girl. So, eat and after you go poop, you can go home tomorrow, because everything works okay."

Emma frowned. "Where's Agnus?"

Max set the bag of clothes beside the bed. "Angus is working at his house, looking at all his fancy new furniture."

Her frown disappeared. "Can I see?"

The men looked relieved at her change of mood. "Tell you what," Max said. "If you're a good girl, I'll see if Angus can make a recording and send it to you on Daddy's phone. That way, you can see him with all his new stuff. And you can send him a funny one back."

She clapped her hands and whooped, making the men smile. The door opened, and a nurse came in with a tray of food for her lunch. "Okay, Emma, that's my cue to move on," the doctor said, closing the door behind him.

Nate said he could manage without assistance, and the nurse left the room. While Emma ate, Max called Angus and asked him to work on the recording. In the meantime, she read her the new book and played cowboys with the toy horse.

When the message arrived an hour later, Nate slipped off to have a quick shower and change. In the meantime, Emma giggled at Angus's outrageous antics. The two of them made a funny one to send back. Shortly after, Emma finally fell asleep, her face finally getting a flush of pink back on her cheeks.

"You look better today," Max said to Nate on his return, seeing his look of strain had eased.

He sat in the chair and nodded. "Doc said she's having a great recovery. The extra night is just a precaution."

"I figured."

"I'll get Angus's table to him tomorrow."

She laughed. "Don't worry about it. I don't think he's too concerned, given the circumstances."

He leaned back and stretched, rolling his shoulders. "So, the furniture arrived, safe and sound?"

"Yes. It arrived this morning. And the countertops, too."

"Oh, yeah. Forgot about them." He yawned. "So, he seemed pleased with everything?"

"Yup. Looked like we'd given him a million bucks."

"Good." He paused. "He's a pretty decent guy, you know."

She stood. "I know." Dropping a kiss on his forehead, she turned to leave. "You comfortable enough for one more night?"

"Yeah. They offered me a rollout cot, but half of me would hang off it, anyway. The chair isn't too bad."

"Okay." She blew Emma a kiss so as not to wake her. "Call me in the morning and let me know when she's going to be released. I'll come and pick you guys up."

Driving back, she stopped at the bakery and bought two stacked deli sandwiches, brimming with meat and cheese for her and Angus. She found him stretching to hold one of the ceiling fans in place while one of the crew adjusted the wiring before putting it into position. After they finished, she said, "Break time," waving his lunch under his nose.

They sat on the new dining room chairs. Since they currently had no table, they used a corner of the work bench to spread the food on instead. She filled him in on Emma's condition, including her rare sulk.

"I don't blame her. I hate being in the hospital."

"Nobody likes being in the hospital."

He swallowed his bite. "Actually, hypochondriacs do."

She poked his arm, clearing her throat to keep from choking. "Don't be so literal."

They finished their meal in companionable silence. Collecting the garbage, Angus said, "We'll have the party in a week, so Emma has enough time to recover."

"Good idea."

"That will give my mother some time to make plans to get here, too."

She nodded. "Better warn you. Emma will pressure you to have cotton candy and balloons. It's her status quo for parties of any description."

He shrugged. "Don't see why not."

"Softie."

"Don't tell her, but after all this drama, she's probably going to get whatever she wants for a while."

She drove over and picked up Nate and Emma at the hospital the next morning. True to his word, the doctor showed up first thing to sign the necessary papers and release her. Emma chattered all the way home, then fell asleep on the couch.

****

Pete sucked back the frosty bottle of beer as he slouched on his tattered recliner at home, following it with a second, then a third. *To hell with work.* Reaching out, he grabbed the picture of Max. Staring at it brought angry tears to his eyes. He'd waited so many years for her, longer than anyone had any right to expect. And he'd had no time at all to celebrate his triumph over Alan.

Then, this morning, he watched as Max and his nemesis exited her house and walked down the hill together. There could be no mistaking the intimacy of the moment.

He'd opened the truck door and thrown up all over the road, then simply driven away. Halfway home, he'd called one of the guys on the job to tell him he was sick and headed for bed.

Shoving his beer bottle onto the table, he walked to where her T-shirt lay on his chair. Grasping it with one hand, he pulled his pocket knife out of his pocket and flicked it open. He shredded the material, stabbing it with angry jerks and sawing through. When he imagined his rival's face on the fabric, his thrusts got stronger, and he raged to the empty room.

## Chapter Fifteen

Making party preparations and easing Emma back into her routine filled the following week. They all kept their eyes on her, watching for any complications, but, luckily, saw none. When Nate needed a break to get some rest, Max and Angus filled in.

In a predictable move, he arranged for the cotton candy machine and cleaned out the town's balloon supply, getting very specific color recommendations from Emma. She directed them all from her makeshift throne on the couch.

Angus did the cooking part of the preparation, making platters of pasta and a huge salad early Saturday morning so they wouldn't be rushed for time. They bought a dozen loaves of French bread from the bakery. Cases of beer, wine, and five kinds of ice cream along with assorted toppings to make sundaes came from the grocery store to complete the dinner.

As everyone helped with the last-minute preparations, Ghost showed up beside the patio as if invited, and they had to shoo him away. Lina, who had arrived that morning, suggested they should welcome him inside and let him join the celebration. As if he knew he had a new admirer, he lingered in the backyard instead of going home. Angus didn't mind, and the dogs were around to keep him company.

Max returned after having a shower to freshen up, dressed in a fresh blouse and jeans. Lina had come downstairs in the meantime, wearing linen pants and a silk blouse, which, according to Angus, was about as casual as she liked to dress. “Darling,” she said, offering her cheek for a kiss. “The house is truly divine.” She beamed up at Angus. “He loves it.”

“Did you get settled in the guestroom?”

Lina nodded, taking a sip of her martini. “It’s charming. I can see your lovely horse from my window.” She gestured to the huge metal tub full of beer in the kitchen. “I’ve never seen that type of container used before. What an efficient idea.”

Nate and Emma arrived then, and Lina, immediately smitten, allowed herself to be taken on a tour. Babbling with excitement, Emma showed her the cotton candy machine Angus had rented and the colorful cluster of balloons next to it.

“Emma seems to like your mom,” Nate said.

Angus smiled. “Everyone does.”

“How long does she plan to stay?”

He shrugged. “I don’t know. As long as she wants. She has an open invitation.”

The crew began showing up with their dates, and the music increased in volume. Angus moved into the kitchen and took trays of food out of the refrigerator to reheat. Emma gave a little yip when she saw her favorite bacon cheese treats come out of the oven and insisted Lina try one. “Oh, you’re right, honey. They’re delicious.”

When Nate disappeared to take Emma to the rest room, Lina turned to Max. “What a delightful child.”

“Yes, she is.”

"And her mother?" Lina raised an eyebrow.

Max sighed. "Her mother has never really been in the picture. She left before Emma turned one."

"That beautiful child is better off without her, then. She doesn't know what she's missing."

Max met her gaze, appreciating the warmth she saw in the other woman's eyes. "That's right. Her loss."

"And her father, well, it's as if you two are siblings. Am I right?"

She nodded. "He's my brother in every way, but blood."

"How wonderful to have such a loving family."

The music suddenly switched to an older song with a slower tempo, which surprised her until Nate made his way through the crowd and asked Lina to dance. She looked startled but said yes and followed him to the center of the room.

Max watched with pleasure as they waltzed around the room, knowing the men would be astounded at Nate's graceful moves. His massive size dwarfed Lina's. The sweetness of the picture they made brought a tear to Max's eye. She looked toward the kitchen to find Angus staring, transfixed at the sight.

She wandered in his direction, catching his eye as she approached. "His mother taught him when he was a little kid."

"My mother is thrilled. She loves to dance."

"Did she teach you?"

He laughed. "Oh, she tried. I'm afraid I'm the proverbial klutz. I can fake it if I have to, I guess."

"Me, too." The song ended. The men clapped and whistled enough to make Nate flush. Emma pushed through the couples to ask her dad to dance with her as

Lina rejoined them. She watched as he lifted Emma, letting her legs dangle as he circled the room.

"What a lovely man." She watched as Max took a photograph with her phone. "Will you send me a copy?"

"Of course."

She turned to her son. "Where is Ian tonight? He is coming, isn't he?"

"He just texted a few minutes ago. He's on his way. I guess he had to help on a call that got a little out of hand."

A few minutes later, their friend appeared at the front door, the beginnings of a bruise framing his left eye causing some sympathetic groans. He grinned. "Like my eye shadow?"

"You have a boo-boo," Emma said, running over to him. "You get a candy to make it better."

"Oh, good. Thanks, honey." Max handed him a beer instead, which he held against his eye for a minute. "Guess what's the number one reason I hate domestic calls?"

"Husband or wife?" Angus asked.

"How did you know?" Ian gave a dramatic groan. "I had the six-foot-two husband under control, but when I went to put him in the squad car, the wife came at me with an umbrella. She's maybe five-foot-two, at the most, but that umbrella sure packed a mean punch."

Everyone laughed, and Max went to get him a bag of ice to reduce the swelling. After relaxing for a while, Ian made the rounds and then sat down with the others to eat. In a rare, quiet moment he asked if anyone had seen Alan Patterson.

When everyone replied in the negative, he explained that Alan had gone missing from his apartment and work. "His father's getting quite concerned."

In another hour or two, the crowd began to thin, people drifting off to go home or to the local bar. Emma had fallen asleep on Nate's lap. Max started to clear some of the serving platters, but Angus took over, joking that he would know how to load the dishwasher better. They had used paper plates and plastic implements for easy cleanup, so those were gathered and thrown into a big garbage bag. Between the two of them, it didn't take long to clear everything away.

"That lasagna tasted wonderful," Lina said. The others agreed.

"I think the second sundae did me in," Ian announced, rubbing his stomach.

"Only two?" Max said. "You must be getting old."

He agreed. "And now this old man's aimed straight to bed." Saying his goodnights, he headed out the door.

Lina excused herself, yawning as she headed up to bed. As Nate went to scoop Emma off the couch where she still lay sleeping, Angus turned to Max. "Why don't you stay here tonight?"

She blushed. "It's just too weird with your mom right across the hall."

"She wouldn't mind."

"I know."

"Okay. I get it. I'll see you tomorrow." He leaned and kissed her on the cheek.

She followed close behind Nate as he made his way out to the truck, her heart pounding as she concentrated on the porch light. She took a seat, and he settled Emma on the seat next to her, started the engine, and switched on the map light. "It'll just take a second, Max. You okay?"

She nodded, the nerves in her neck cramping as she tried to focus on Emma. He sped up the hill, coming to a halt right beside her porch. She slipped out from beneath Emma, laying her head gently down.

Escorting Max inside, he flipped on the hall light for her as she breathed a grateful sigh. She hugged him and closed the door behind him, locking it. Watching them through the window as they drove past the house, she heard the crackle of the gravel as they continued to his place. He'd become used to all these finicky procedures for the rare occasions when she went out at night, but it didn't make asking him to do it any less embarrassing.

****

Angus sat in the sunny kitchen sipping his morning coffee. Surprised to see his mother coming down the stairs, already dressed, he said, "You're up early for a party girl."

She smiled and took a seat at the island. "I'm old, and time is slipping by. I don't want to miss anything. The bed is lovely, though, especially those wonderful linens."

The sheets had been thanks to Max. He'd almost forgotten he needed a set for the guest room. "I'm glad you found it comfortable. What can I make you for breakfast?"

"Oh, tea and toast will do."

He pushed away from the counter and stood. "How about a nice omelet?"

"Don't go to any trouble."

He laughed. “You know me. The last thing you ever have to worry about is a shortage of food.” Reaching into the refrigerator, he removed the required ingredients. “Swiss cheese, tomatoes, and bacon okay?”

“It sounds divine.” She rose from her stool and moved to fill the kettle. “I had so much fun at your party. Your friends are lovely.”

“Thanks. I’m glad you enjoyed it.”

“Nate’s little Emma is a jewel.”

“She is, indeed, the treasure of the neighborhood.” He whisked the eggs and milk. “What would you like to do today?”

“If you have some time available, I thought that perhaps you could show me more of your little town.”

“I’d love to.” He added some herbs and poured the eggs into the pan. “Any place in particular you’d like to go?”

She slipped back onto her seat. “Max mentioned a farmer’s market. It sounded quite charming.”

“It is,” he replied. “They have everything from furniture to the best baked goods I’ve tasted.”

“Why don’t we see if Max wants to come along?”

He stifled a grin at the casual question. It amused him that his mother thought she could manage his love life. “Sure. I’ll text her and see if she’s up. She sometimes sleeps in on Saturdays.” The boiling kettle whistled, and he made her a pot of tea.

Max didn’t answer his text, so he left a message about where they were going in case she wanted to join them later. He gave his mother a driving tour of the town, and they circled back to the market.

They had been strolling around the stalls for an hour or so when they heard a high-pitched squeal.

Emma roared down the lane toward them, legs pumping, dodging other customers like a miniature linebacker. “I found them,” she shrieked, and he laughed as Nate jogged to catch up, Max bringing up the rear.

Emma hugged his leg. “I get a treat, ’cause I found you first.”

“That’s only fair.” He ruffled her hair, making her giggle.

She grinned up at his mother. “Are you my Lina?” she asked.

Confused, Angus’s mother looked at the others. “What do you mean, honey?” her dad asked.

Emma gave an indignant frown. “He’s my Agnus. Does that mean she’s my Lina?”

Lina leaned over and smoothed Emma’s hair. “I would love to be your Lina, if that’s okay with your dad.”

“Course.” Her frown eased, and she touched Angus’s and Lina’s arms. “Now, I have a daddy and a Max and a Agnus and a Lina. I have the mostest people in the world.”

“Yes, you do.” Lina dug in her purse for a hankie and dabbed away a tear. “Now, you need to help me find the special cookies my son keeps talking about.”

After a while, they stopped for a lunch break. Angus laughed when his mother took way too long figuring out how to safely navigate the monster sandwiches they purchased, stuffed with meat, cheese, and fresh vegetables. She ended up pulling it apart and tackling it with a plastic knife and fork. The big cups of fresh-squeezed lemonade were everyone’s favorite.

Later, on their way out, they found their favorite cookie baker, and everyone bought a supply of her wares. "How do you manage to stay slim here?" Lina asked.

"We don't," they answered in unison, making Emma shout, "Jinx."

They said their goodbyes in the parking lot, splitting off in different directions. His mother remained unusually quiet on the way back to the house. "Are you okay?" he asked.

"Of course," she answered. "You really are very happy here, aren't you?"

"I am. Surprisingly so. Are you comfortable with that?"

Leaning over, she patted his arm. "I'm thrilled for you, actually. I didn't understand at first, but I do now." She cleared her throat. "Can I have a mother moment?"

"Of course."

"Do you hope to have children some day? I know we've never talked about it, but I just wondered. You seemed so comfortable with little Emma."

He realized, with a start, she was right. They had never discussed it. "I would like to, yes, if it works out."

"Oh, I'm so glad. Having you was the best thing that ever happened to me. I would like you to have the same experience, if possible."

He smiled. "Of course, hoping and having it come true might be two different things."

"I'll think positive thoughts."

"Fair enough."

His mother went home to Louisville after three days, saying she didn't want him to get bored of her company, because she'd be back. He spent the rest of the day getting used to the house and returning the motor home. Nate picked him up at the dealership, and then they swung around to pick up Emma from school.

"Your mom is pretty fabulous, by the way," Nate said as he pulled into the driveway and came to a stop.

"Thanks. She really enjoyed herself."

He gestured toward the house. "Does it feel like home yet?"

Angus laughed. "Sort of. I keep dreaming I'm going to wake up and it'll be back the way it used to be." He unbelted and then paused. "How's the new project going?"

"Not as smooth as yours, so far." He rubbed his face. "The new owners have a habit of second-guessing every decision. It makes for long days."

"Poor Max. At least you can do a lot of your part from home."

"Thank goodness."

He got out and waved goodbye, laughing at Emma as she wiggled out of her seatbelt to dangle out to return his wave. Nate leaned over to grab her coat for safety.

Walking up the stairs, he noted how quiet the house seemed now, with all the work finished. The house appeared almost too big after the trailer, but he knew getting used to all this space would take some time. Better too much room than too little. He'd spent enough years in apartments.

Max hadn't been around after the farmer's market. He hoped she was just giving him some space to spend time with his mother.

## Chapter Sixteen

Ian showed up on Angus's steps the following morning. He let him into the house, led the way to the kitchen, and handed him a cup of coffee. "What's up?"

"Can you lend me some of your legendary brain power this morning?"

"Sure. What do you need?"

"I'm afraid I might have figured out where Todd is. I thought he might have broken down and found some suspicious tracks up on Cliff Road. I know it's not your specialty or anything, but I just need another set of eyes and an objective opinion."

He turned to stare. "You think he might have gone over the edge?"

"Maybe. He uses that road more than most of the locals do. If you agree it looks suspicious, I need to find out how to get a look down into the valley below."

Leaving their coffee behind, they headed that way, arriving fifteen minutes later. They parked down the road a bit, in a lay-by, for safety. Hiking back up to the blind curve, Ian pointed to the disturbed dirt. "You see, we have one set of tracks that look like a truck. The second set is from a car."

"I see it." Angus squatted down on his heels to get a better look. "An expensive tire on the car by the look of the tread." Standing, he followed them to where the two sets almost connected.

Ian shifted from foot to foot. "To me, it looks like they almost collided, then the car swerved. Am I right?"

Angus studied them from both sides and every angle. "Yes. No doubt about it. And the tracks go right off the edge." The most likely theory troubled him. "I'm a little hesitant to say this, but this looks intentional. Like a game of chicken that went wrong."

"So, I'm not crazy." He blew out a frustrated breath. "How the hell am I going to get down there and check to see if we're right?"

Angus took a moment to consider, peering down the steep embankment. "Know anybody with a drone?"

"Son of a bitch. That's a great idea." He slapped him on the shoulder. "I do, thank goodness." He got on his cellphone and, thirty minutes later, the friend showed up with his equipment.

They watched, fascinated, as he sent the drone down into the canyon. It took mere minutes to locate the wreckage, wedged partially under a thick stand of trees. Alan appeared to be deceased, his body slumped across the front seat. EMTs were called to be certain, along with a few local climbers who could assist with recovery. The procedure took hours. Angus hung around to suggest what pictures they should take to help with proving someone had intentionally caused the tragedy.

Ian dropped him back at his house on his way to notify Alan's father. "My least favorite job," he muttered, wiping his dusty face on his sleeve.

Angus filled Max in after she got home. She blanched. "Oh, I feel awful. His poor father. I didn't like Alan, but nobody deserves such an awful death. Who would do such a thing?"

"No idea. We'll probably never find out. All Ian has is the photographs of those tire tracks. We didn't find any other evidence."

A few evenings later, Angus saw Nate and Emma playing on their lawn with Max's dogs and he wandered over. Ghost followed his progress along the fence line as far as he could, then settled down to graze. As he approached, Emma shrieked and waved, appearing to herd the dogs into a corner.

"What's she doing?" he asked.

Nate laughed. "Playing cowgirl. It's her latest thing. She herds them into a corner for branding." They watched as she picked up a small branch, pointing it like a branding iron. "Take it easy with the stick," he shouted.

"It's just pretend," she answered, grinning as she waved it over her head and ran after them.

"Wish I had that kind of energy." Angus slipped through the fence to join him. "I didn't mean to interrupt. I was curious about something and thought I'd ask you about it."

"Shoot."

"What happened to Max's mom? She told me she died, but I got the impression there might be more to the story than that. I just didn't want to put her on the spot."

Nate sighed. "Someone murdered her when Max was ten."

It took a minute to absorb the words. "Murdered? By whom?"

"They never found out for sure, although almost everybody thought it could be her father." He met Angus's gaze. "Her old man was in prison for white collar crime when he died but swore he didn't do it. The sheriff at the time didn't think he did, either, but the case went unsolved."

"I can't imagine what that experience must have been like for her."

"It wasn't easy. She became a strong woman despite it, though."

"Was her mother killed at home?"

"Yeah. Max escaped and hid in the woods behind the house until the cops came."

"I can't believe she was so close when such a tragic thing happened. It must have been terrifying."

"Yeah. She lived the next eight years in an orphanage, but at least we still went to the same school. She was considered unadoptable, because she couldn't sleep through the night, even with therapy."

"That's hardly a surprise. Thanks for telling me. It explains a lot."

Nate shrugged. "She would have told you sooner or later. She has some trust issues about the really personal stuff."

Emma broke the moment with loud whoops of joy. "Yeehaw." The dogs escaped and trotted toward the men, looking tuckered out.

"Come on, Em. Time to get ready for bed."

"Ah, Daddy." She ran up and hugged Angus's leg. "But I didn't talk to Agnus yet."

"There's always tomorrow."

Her lip came out, but she said goodnight and followed her father. Angus gave Ghost another pat as he passed by and headed home.

****

Max dragged through her front door, a takeout pizza in one hand. She had grime smeared from nostrils to toenails. Residual sweat mixed with it, causing her skin to stick to her clothes. Tossing her dinner on the counter, she headed right for the shower. Peeling off the gritty clothes, she threw them right into the washing machine. Measuring out detergent, she switched it on.

Twenty minutes later, the accumulated dirt had trailed down the drain, but her energy still sunk to an all-time low. She shoved her tired, aching limbs into soft pajamas and drank a glass of milk, refilling it before she stopped to reheat the pizza. At least the enticing aroma of meat and cheese heating had replaced the memorable, sweaty fragrance of an exhausting day.

The headache which had plagued her all day still hammered at her skull, so she shook out a few painkillers and gulped them down. She replayed the day in her head. *No, ma'am, I can't find you that fancy tile at half price. No, sir, you can't move in before the house is finished.*

Common sense just didn't seem common anymore. She had just begun eating her pizza when the phone buzzed. She ignored it. When it buzzed again, she kept chewing and read the text on the screen. *Angus*.

—How was your day?—

She thought of all the tempting cuss words she could use, but instead said, "Crappy."

After a minute's delay, he answered.

—Nate said your new folks are difficult. Got a headache?—

Now he could read her over the phone. *More than a little daunting*. —Yes.—

A pause, then,

—Get some rest and a decent dinner. I'll catch you tomorrow.—

Maybe she wanted him to come to her door and ask to be let in. Maybe she didn't. Hell, what did she want?

That made it the question of the hour, didn't it? What did she want from Angus?

Max had left him to spend time with his mother, which made sense, but had led to an appalling conclusion.

She missed him. A mere two or three days apart and she had missed seeing him during the day, poking his stupid nerd head around the corner when she least expected it.

Since her mother died, she had never needed anybody but Nate and Emma. Oh, she wanted him, no question about that. Hot, steamy dreams caused her to thrash around in bed instead of sleep. That had been part of the source of her headache. She wanted a repeat of their passionate night together, but how would that indulgence complicate things? If he acted like more of a jerk, this wouldn't be a problem.

Why couldn't he be a jerk, like so many men she'd encountered through the years? That would clarify her options in a flash.

Blowing out a frustrated breath, she flaked onto the couch, keeping the pizza and milk on the end table within easy reach. She nibbled off and on while watching a few television programs. Sleep finally came, shortly after three, born of sheer exhaustion.

When she woke at six, at least her pounding headache had abated. Downing more pain killers would prevent a recurrence. Taking her time, she fed the animals, had a cool shower, and prepared to face another day of customer complaints.

Thank goodness, the soon-to-be owners were nowhere to be found when she arrived at the site. She checked in with everyone, pleased to see excellent progress was being made. The sooner they were finished with these people, the better.

Nate was checking the measurements for the built-ins when his phone rang. He listened for a minute, then Max heard him say the name of their local doctor. She walked over and mouthed, Emma, and he shook his head. "No, call me back if you can get an appointment. I'll come and drive you over." Pausing, he said, "Don't be an idiot. It's not safe." He hung up. "Angus pulled a back muscle, and he's pretty much the walking dead. He's going to text me if he can get an appointment with the doctor and I'll drive him."

"Shouldn't I go with you?"

"Nah." He offered the glimmer of a smile. "He'll feel embarrassed enough as it is. Macho crap. You chicks wouldn't understand."

She punched him on the arm as his phone buzzed. "Good," he said, tapping in an answer. "Doc said he'll see him right away, so I'm off to pick him up. Probably be an hour or two before I get back."

"Okay."

Nate had already been gone for thirty minutes when the female owner showed up with more pictures from a design magazine for Max to inspect. Stifling a groan, she took some time listening to her rave about the elegant presentation. She then had to break it to her that they would have to almost double their budget for the same look.

The sulky frown on the woman's face was becoming too familiar. Yesterday, she had actually said, "Pretty please," about something and Max had almost asked her if she was twelve. A patient woman herself, she worried that the client might have an absolute temper tantrum next, complete with stamping feet and bunched fists.

Most of the time, she preferred to build or remodel homes, then sell, rather than build for specific people because of customers like her. This sale had worked into their schedule well, though, and meant money flowing in the door. It kept her workers occupied. If she didn't keep them working, they might migrate to someone else's company that could, and a great team took time to build.

Nate returned from his errand of mercy about one p.m. after she'd gulped down a sandwich she'd brought from home. "Well, he's doped to the gills with muscle relaxants and was falling asleep on the couch when I left him."

"Couldn't make the stairs up to his bedroom?"

He shook his head. "Never seen him grouchy before. It's kinda funny."

"Did you at least leave him something to eat and drink?"

"Yes, Mom. I put a sandwich and some juice on the coffee table next to him, but I think he's going to sleep first." He grinned. "He cussed at me."

"You probably deserved it."

He shrugged. "I just called him Grandpa."

"That's mean." She chuckled. "Funny, but mean."

"I told him we'd check in with him after work to make sure he's doing okay. He said, good, that by then he'd need someone to bury him."

It amused her how insulted men always were at pain. She figured women had better tolerance, but that would be an opinion she'd keep to herself for the moment.

At three p.m., Nate left to pick up Emma from school, and all three met at the steps of Angus's house. They were quiet on entering, but he was already awake, staring at the television, hunched awkwardly on his side.

Emma tiptoed in first. "Agnus, are you sick? Dad says you have an owie."

He gave a smile that turned into more of a grimace. "Dad's right about that, honey."

"Are you broke?"

Now, he smiled. "Not for good, Emma. Just for a few days."

She looked down at the half-eaten sandwich. "That looks yucky."

"It's okay. I'm not very hungry, anyway."

She looked up at Max. "Can we make him soup? Dad says eating soup is good for you when you're sick."

"Sure." She inspected his covers. "No heating pad?"

"Don't have one," he growled.

Max turned to Nate. "Go get my heating pad out of the bathroom cupboard. Top shelf. Emma and I will make him some soup." Ignoring the expected protests from the patient, she headed for the kitchen.

She found enough ingredients in the kitchen to throw together some chicken vegetable soup, letting it bubble on the stove for a while. When Nate returned, she took the heating pad from him, plugging it into a nearby outlet and setting the control. "Just lean forward two or three inches so I can wiggle it to the right spot." Angus grumbled but did as directed. Afterward, she took the opposite seat. "When are your next pain pills due?"

"They're not working worth a damn, anyway. Why bother?"

She hid a grin. "It'll get better. They take a couple of doses to kick in." Picking up the bottle, she twisted off the cap and shook two pills into her hand. She said to Nate, "Last dose around noon?"

"Closer to one," he answered.

She dug up a writing pad to note the times, then fetched him a glass of water to take his next dose. "Always write down when you take your dose, then you know when you're due."

Angus muttered something that sounded like a curse, gulped down the pills, and pulled the blanket up around his neck with only his head poking out. He looked like the giant brother of a snapping turtle.

"Don't get too comfy. I'm getting you some soup to eat."

"I don't want any soup."

She chuckled. "Tough boots. You have to eat something with that medication or you'll get nauseated. That's a combo you shouldn't volunteer for." Dishing up the aromatic broth, she turned off the burner while Emma added crackers to the plate. They carried it over to where he lay on the sofa, setting it down on the coffee table in the vicinity of his nose.

He opened one eye, sighed, and reached for the spoon. Carefully propping himself up on one arm, he ate one spoonful, then two.

"See, Agnus, it's yummy," Emma said. "Me and Max made it just for you."

She watched as her pint-sized assistant walked over and planted a kiss on the side of Angus's head. "Okay, you guys. Time to go. I think our patient needs some sleep."

"Nighty, night, sleep tight," Emma said in a singsong voice and joined the other two as they left.

"I'll check on you a little later," Max called before she shut the door.

He grunted in response.

When she came back to check three hours later, he eased himself to a sitting position, his blanket sliding to the floor. "Feeling any better?"

"Marginally." He made a feeble attempt to tidy his hair, which stuck up in every direction.

"What can I get you?"

He gave a dramatic sigh. "If you can figure out how to pee for me, that would help."

Max laughed. "Well, that's beyond my powers, I'm afraid. How about I start you in the right direction?" She helped him ease up from the sofa to a standing position and propped herself under one arm. They shuffled down the hall to the guest bathroom, and she leaned in to flick on the light. "Can you manage from here?"

"Yes. No further indignities required. Just stay close."

A few minutes later, mission accomplished, they were hobbling back. She inspected his back and removed the heating pad. "But that feels good," he protested. His tone reminded her of Emma in the hospital.

"You can have it back in a little while. Your back is too red right now. You don't want a burn." She let him settle back down, propping his back with a pillow.

He looked past her through the front windows. "It'll be dark soon."

"Yes."

"Can you stay here tonight?"

"If you want me to. I'd have to get the dogs. Is that okay?"

"Of course." He stuffed the pillow beneath his head. "Go get what you need now, so you'll be back before the sun goes down."

"Okay."

When she reached the door, she heard a mumbled, "Thanks."

Max grabbed some pajamas and a fresh change of clothes while the dogs ate. She took a detour to feed Ghost on her way back down the hill. Confused, the dogs trotted behind her, looking around, then darting up the steps after her when they arrived. Shushing them, she peeked in and saw he'd fallen asleep.

She let herself in, telling them to lay down by the front window. Settling into the chair, she texted Nate that she'd appointed herself Angus's nurse for the night so he wouldn't worry when he didn't see the lights on at her house.

Angus snored and grumbled in his sleep which made her smile, thinking about Nate's grandpa crack.

At midnight, her patient woke. They made a repeat trip down the hall, and she doled out another set of pills. When he settled, she dug up a blanket from his linen closet and curled up in the recliner across from him. The dogs lay down between them.

## Chapter Seventeen

Angus woke to find the morning sun peeping through the curtains, momentarily confused until his back throbbed and memory returned. His roving gaze found Max curled up in the leather chair, her hair pooled around her shoulders. Hurt back or not, he experienced a surge of attraction he would have to ignore for now. The fact that all three of them had cared enough to help him out touched him.

A quick glance around showed she had only left two lamps on. Why hadn't she turned on all the lights like she did at home? He remembered her giving him the pills at midnight. The clock read six-thirty now. Had she slept all night?

She stirred. When she woke, the dogs rose and stretched, looking around. "Morning," she said, stretching out in every direction like a star.

"Hey," he said. "Did you get some sleep?"

She sat up. "I guess so. What time is it?"

"Six-thirty."

"You're kidding." She rubbed her face. "I slept in. How are you feeling?"

"Better. The muscle relaxants finally kicked in." The dogs came up and licked his face. "Well, good morning to you, too," he said, grimacing.

She called them off, laughing. Standing, she gave each one a pat. "Want me to get you some cereal?"

"Bathroom first." He waved away her attempts to help. "Let's see if I can manage on my own." It took him a few minutes, but he made it there and returned, hunched over and shuffling. "Kind of pathetic that I feel a small sense of achievement for something any five-year-old can do."

She set the box of cereal down in front of him with a small jug of milk beside it. Adding a bowl and spoon meant he would be all set. "What else do you need before I head off to work?"

"I think I'm good for now."

"How about a shower?"

He quirked an eyebrow. "Are you implying I need one or offering to join me?"

"You're awfully ambitious for a man who can barely walk."

Angus groaned as he settled back on the sofa. "A man can dream, can't he?" He smiled. "I'll take one later. Thanks for the help. I owe you one."

"No problem. Slap that heating pad on for a while to keep your muscles warm, and call or text if you need anything."

"Lean down for a minute." When she did, he kissed her. "Have a good day."

"I will." Calling the dogs, she headed out.

****

Max counted the final minutes until they finished this house, the clock actually ticking in her head. She hoped she would never see this woman again. The owner-to-be sat on the porch waiting for her and that couldn't be a good sign. "Good morning," she called as she climbed out of the truck, hoping her words would magically make it so.

"I wish I could say it was a good morning," the woman answered, a habitual pout marring her face.

"What's the matter?" she asked, expecting an inevitable complaint about some trivial detail. Mounting the steps, she tried not to drag her feet.

She waved Max inside with dramatic flair, her heels tapping an insistent beat on the tile floor as they entered the kitchen. "I can't believe my eyes," she said, sweeping one arm toward the wall above the counter. Max saw the good progress that had been made the previous day. The backsplash had tiles in place with the grout yet to be added.

"I don't understand your concern. The tile is in place as it should be, and the grout will be completed next to finish the job."

"It looks messy, not at all the way I envisioned it."

Here's what you can do with your visions, she thought, but kept her expression calm. "It isn't complete. When it is, it will be lovely."

"My friend, Todd, says it doesn't look like quality work and that I should demand it be redone. He's a professional."

Everything suddenly became clearer. "Would that be Todd Priestly?"

She nodded, flipping her hair with a smug grin. "Yes, of course. He's an old friend."

From her reaction, she could only guess what kind of friend he'd been. Apparently, even fresh out of the hospital, he was determined to cause trouble. "Well, I'm sorry to have to tell you this, but I fired your friend for poor workmanship. This is simply his way of getting back at me. He's a plumber, not a tile specialist."

The other woman lifted her rather pointed nose and narrowed her eyes, which had the unfortunate effect of making her look like an outraged chicken. "He said you'd be bitter about it because he didn't have any interest in you as a woman."

Now, Max laughed, not caring anymore if she offended her. "I'm not going to argue about this with you. To be blunt, Todd is not allowed on this property until our work is done and you have taken possession." She walked past her. "Now, you'll have to excuse me. I have work to do."

After the wife stormed down the front steps and leapt into her car, Max breathed a sigh of relief. It bothered her that Todd had been mouthing off, possibly inciting his troublemaker friends. Time to post a night guard again, she thought, sighing at the additional expense.

Another unwelcome thought crossed her mind. Is it possible that Todd or one of his crowd had played tricks on her, moving things around in her house? She took out her always growing to-do list. Time to get Nate to change the locks on her house. That way, if she hadn't lost her grip and someone really had been meddling, it would stop. And, if she was wrong, Nate would just think her a little paranoid. She could live with that.

The long workday ended a little more peacefully than it started when the husband buyer called and apologized for his wife's behavior. "She's a little high-strung," he explained. She would bet it wasn't the first time he'd had to offer apologies for his wife's arrogant attitude. Reassuring him, she told him not to worry, thanking him for the call.

As they were packing up for the day, she said to Nate, "Can you change my locks for me sometime this week? I think I'd feel better not taking chances."

"Sure. Be glad to."

Pete dropped his toolbox and walked over. "Don't bother, Nate. I'd be glad to do that for her."

"Thanks, anyway, Pete." She tried to ease her stated preference with a smile. "Nate can take care of it. You have a nice evening."

****

The following day, Angus met Max on her driveway after work. "I saw Nate working on your locks this morning. Is something wrong?"

She tried, and failed, to shove the overwhelming sense of fatigue away. "Not wrong, exactly. I'm doing it for my own peace of mind. I've found a few things moved around in my house lately. It's probably just my poor memory, but I don't want to take the chance."

"Why didn't you tell me?"

He sounded so aggrieved that it rubbed her the wrong way. "Because I don't have to report to you, Angus. I can take care of it."

"I didn't mean to imply that you couldn't. I just—"

"I don't have time to talk about it." Walking around him, she unlocked the door, barely turning to mumble a goodnight before she closed the door behind her.

She refused to feel guilty, she thought later, flipping the television from one channel to the next. Any grown woman who couldn't take care of herself should be horsewhipped. Rubbing her face, she realized that she hadn't really done that, having asked Nate to help her. She should have damn well changed the locks herself.

*Damn it.* Relationships were hard.

Angus didn't deserve to get hit with the brunt of her temper, caused mostly by exhaustion. And that knowledge wouldn't help her sleep tonight, either.

*Great*. The revolving door of exhaustion insisted on smacking her on the ass.

Early the next morning, unable to stomach any breakfast, she walked over to apologize and found his house empty. A phone call to Nate didn't help as he hadn't seen or heard from him. An apology over the phone just didn't have the same impact, so she would have to wait.

## Chapter Eighteen

Angus drove back from the city, racking his brain, wondering how to mend fences with Max. He didn't mean to overstep, he was just concerned about her safety. Sometimes, he had to remind himself that rushing in to try and save the day might not be the best idea.

*Did she really have an intruder?*

He had watched her work. She had a meticulous way of doing business. Did a woman like that ever misplace things? He didn't think so. Not often, anyway.

Ian had called and filled him in about Max's concern for his whereabouts.

Today marked the first day his back had been close to normal, close enough at least to carry out his list of errands. He'd spent a lot of time thinking about the attack on Todd and Alan's suspicious demise, and it troubled him. He put the two things together alongside Max's concerns and her history, all adding up to an unlikely coincidence.

What the hell was going on in this normally peaceful town?

****

Pleasantly surprised to get a phone call from Lina asking her to lunch, Max thought the timing might be perfect. She needed a break. Nate agreed to watch the work site for her and keep things rolling. Lina chose a restaurant about halfway in between their homes to make it a reasonable drive for both of them.

Max looked it up online and found it quite fancy compared to the places where she normally ate. *Not much of a surprise*. She dug a feminine blouse and skirt out of the closet, feeling like a different person when she put them on. Taking the time to put on some makeup, a rarity, seemed like an inordinate waste of time. She didn't want to stand out like a country bumpkin in such proper surroundings, though.

The hour-long drive relaxed her, and the tension eased out of her shoulders, bit by bit. Maybe she needed a masseuse. At least the sun had made an appearance after several days of rain. She could smell the latest cutting of hay through the open window, waiting in the pastures to be baled.

The elegant restaurant, when she found it, nestled next to a picturesque lake. Small boats dotted the surface. She followed the meandering stone path to a beautifully crafted wooden door that had trees carved into it. On entering, she spotted Lina seated at a small table in front of the panoramic window, gazing out. When she approached, the other woman stood, beaming. "There's my girl."

The kind greeting brought a tear to her eye. She brushed it away, mortified, and leaned down to kiss her cheek. "Thanks for inviting me. I know you had a longer drive than I did."

She sat and Max joined her. "Don't you worry about that. After all, I just sat back and read a good book." Leaning in, she touched her hand. "You look so pretty."

"You, too." She meant it. How did the woman look so put together all of the time? "Thanks for the invitation. I really needed a break. I just hope I don't fall asleep halfway through our meal."

Lina laughed. "Don't worry. I'll wake you up if you do." She waved a waiter over with a flick of her hand. "They have the most divine raspberry iced tea here."

"Sounds perfect."

She ordered the drinks. After the waiter left, she asked, "Do you know why I invited you here?"

"Not especially, but the timing was perfect. Sometimes it's nice to escape for a few hours."

"I wanted to get to know you better, but I also have a favor to ask of you."

Max tried to imagine what she could do for a woman that has everything, chauffeur included. "A favor?"

"I need you to forgive my son."

A flush stole up her cheeks. "I will. I already tried to talk to him, but he wasn't home."

"I know. He came to see me first thing this morning."

"I'm surprised he told you. It's not that big of a deal."

The waiter delivered their tea, and she worried about breaking the delicate flowered china. Lina took a sip. "My son is a very practical man. He can't always see the virtue of giving a person breathing room. And he's a man, which is always a bothersome complication."

Her comment made Max chuckle. "I can't keep up with his brain sometimes."

"Oh, darling, not many of us can. And at least his intentions are always good. I do like that he is a protective soul, but sometimes he tries to take the lead when he shouldn't."

Max took a drink, surprised she liked the refreshing taste. "The truth is, I was just overtired and not very fit to see anyone. And I'm so used to taking care of myself."

"I understand. It's a good thing to be independent." They paused to order lunch, each picking a different salad. "I'll tell you a story that might help you understand him a little better. After my husband died, a man in my club started making advances. I thought it quite silly, but it lifted my spirits in a way. He was suave and sophisticated, but clearly after my money. I knew that, but Angus quietly cornered him and, well, I don't know what he said, but the man disappeared, looking quite worried." She smiled. "I couldn't help but feel quite loved and protected, even though that man was never a real threat to me."

"He's always very observant about what's happening around him."

"Oh, yes. It's his best trait."

They talked, then, of other things, and when Lina got around to asking her about her family, she found herself telling her everything. At the end, Lina reached across the table to squeeze her fingers. "Oh, my dear. I'm speechless." She met her gaze. "Does Angus know?"

"Not unless someone else told him."

Clearing her throat, she said, "It explains so much about your concerns. Consider telling him about it. I think you'll both feel much better about the relationship between the two of you."

She considered Lina's advice all of the way home. And she thought about how strange it was to be so comfortable with a woman so different from herself. Still exhausted, she suddenly had more hope for the future than she'd had in a very long time.

****

Pete had a hard time masking the glee that bubbled up after dispatching Alan. He kept replaying the way the car had looked flying off the cliff edge over and over in his mind.

That asshole wouldn't be bothering anyone for eternity, especially Max.

He wished something similar could be done with Angus, but the height difference between them made most attacks next to impossible. Still, there were a lot of ways he could have an accident.

Couldn't be with a car. Been there, done that. Not a great idea to create a pattern. It cheered him, though, to consider each possible scenario.

Whistling as he worked, he wondered about which method to pick. Some rat poison in his coffee, maybe, or a fire to burn down his new house? Fun to think about, it made the day pass in a celebratory blur.

****

After Max arrived home, she wasted some time practicing her apology, then took a big breath and headed down to Angus's house. She dragged herself up the steps, muttering to herself, and heard the door creak open. He stood in the doorway.

She started with the basics. "Hi."

"Hi, yourself. I was just on my way up to see you." Opening the door wider, he gestured for her to come inside. He slid onto one of the barstools in the kitchen, and she followed suit. Turning to face her, he said, "I owe you an apology."

She shook her head. "I'm the one who should apologize. I tore your head off just because I let myself get too overtired."

"Well, I meant to show concern about your welfare, but I stuck my nose in where it didn't belong."

She shrugged. "Can we just wave a truce flag and be done with it?"

"That would be great." He smiled. "Did you take a drive to blow off some steam?"

"I had lunch with your mom." She chuckled when she saw the look of surprise on his face. "It really helped me to talk to her, you know. She's pretty amazing."

"She is indeed. She didn't waste any time, either. I just saw her first thing this morning."

"I know. She mentioned that. The thing is, she just said a few words and I found myself spilling my guts to her."

"That's how it usually happens. It's her gift."

She sucked in a breath. "She said there were some things I should tell you about my past. Things that might help you understand me better."

Leaning over, he kissed her forehead. "I know about your mom, Max. Nate told me the other day."

"Oh. I didn't realize he'd said anything."

"Well, to tell you the truth, I asked. I can't imagine what that experience must be like, but I'm incredibly proud of you. You survived it and moved forward with your life. Not everyone could do that."

"It's had an effect on me."

"How could it not?"

"My fear of the night might never go away, you know."

He nodded. "That's true. It may not. But there are some things we could try together that might help, if you're willing to investigate a few options."

"I already tried drugs. I didn't like the way they made me feel. It's like I sleepwalked through my days."

"I'm not talking about drugs. I'm talking about some form of behavior modification."

She considered it for a moment. "I've never tried that."

"I thought we might try a form of desensitization. Like going outside at night for a minute at a time and then building up from there."

"Why didn't anyone suggest that before?"

"I don't know, but I've actually given this a lot of thought. I certainly think it's worth a try."

"Is that something your scientific brain conjured up in your spare time?"

He nodded, chuckling. "It's a therapy that's had some success with troubled children and animals. Why not you? It's what I would try if I were in your position."

A glimmer of hope moved through her. "I'll give it some serious thought. Thanks."

"Now, on to more practical things. Have you eaten dinner?"

"No."

"Want to stay and eat with me?"

"Can I go home, have a nice, warm, soaky bath and come back?"

"Of course. It will take some time to prepare, anyway. What do you feel like?"

"You pick."

"I was considering baked chicken, mashed potatoes, and fresh corn."

"That sounds perfect." She took his face in her hands and kissed him. "I'll be back in a while."

Tempted to run uphill to have her bath, she couldn't believe how much better their talk made her feel. Now, she just wanted to freshen up, relax a bit, and head right back down to him.

Once she and the dogs were inside the house, she laid some fresh clothes on the bed. Leaving the dogs to wander around, she ran the bath, adding some bubbles just for fun. When she heard them bark, she walked out to check the trees the dogs were fixated on, only to find a couple of squirrels bickering. "They're not bothering you," she scolded the three of them. "Settle down."

Taking off her clothes, she threw them in the hamper. She had just slipped into the water, feeling the warmth surround her, when they barked again. "I'm not getting out," she called. "Go lay down." She heard them scuffle a bit, then silence.

She stretched out, wiggling her toes and letting the water relax her muscles. Picking up her flowered washcloth and scented soap, she rubbed lazy circles on her arms. After a languid scrub over her whole body, she relaxed again. She stole a few secret moments to consider what might happen between her and Angus after dinner.

Leaning back in the bathtub, her eyes closed, she heard a floorboard squeak. "Nate?" she called, sitting up and opening her eyes.

*No answer.*

Knowing her imagination likely played tricks on her, she climbed out of the clawfoot tub and grabbed her terry robe from the hook on the back of the door. *Where are the dogs?* She couldn't hear them. Had they fallen asleep?

She slipped on the robe, belting it. As she went into the hall, she could hear the dogs' muffled barks. Trailing droplets of water to the tile floor, she peeked around the corner, feeling foolish.

Sucking in a breath of surprise, she pulled the edges of her robe closed, staring. "Pete, what's wrong? What are you doing here?"

Standing in the open doorway of the kitchen as if he had every right to be there, he gave a caricature of a smile, his lips stretched too thin. He stood as if braced against some unseen enemy. "Where else would I be, Max? I've been at your beck and call for years, right? Why would today be any different?"

Her heart chose an uneasy rhythm as she struggled to comprehend her situation. "You've worked for me for years, yes." His manic expression gave her pause. "And I think we've been friends all of that time, haven't we?"

"Friends?" He spat the word out as if it tasted like arsenic, his face reddening. "I don't want to be your friend, Max."

"I'm afraid I d-don't understand." Wrapping her arms around herself, she attempted to stay calm.

One of the dogs gave a distant bark. She realized with a spurt of alarm he must have penned them in the spare bedroom. As her mind ramped up to speed, she realized he wore black clothing, head to toe, like a burglar. She took a deep breath to calm herself, letting it trickle out from between her lips. “Tell me what’s going on with you, Pete. We can sit down and talk about it.”

He shook his head. “The time for talk is long past, Max. And that’s your fault. You brought this to a head when you chose him instead of me.”

“Chose who?”

“Dr. Big Shot.” Pete shoved his hands on his hips, puffing out his chest. “Why him? He shows up out of nowhere and everyone makes such a fuss, even you. He’s nothing special, Max. He’ll drop you like a brick when someone better comes along.”

*What do I say to stop this? What could possibly talk him down from this cliff?* She softened her tone. “I’m sorry if I hurt you, Pete. I didn’t know you had feelings for me.”

“How could you not know?” he shouted, flailing his arms for emphasis. “I did everything you ever asked of me. And so much more.” He paced back and forth, muttering under his breath. She searched for an opportunity to run past him, but he blocked the only access.

*Can I shove past him?*

“I did everything I could think of to show that you need a real man to take care of you.”

Enlightenment broke through her confusion. “You’re the one who kept moving things around and leaving my door open.”

A maniacal grin spread on his face. “It should have worked.” Then his face twisted. “But it didn’t, did it? And you asked Nate to change your locks. I couldn’t allow you to shut me out.”

Reaching into his pocket, he pulled out a pistol, and she gasped as he waved it in her direction. “I guess I finally got your attention, didn’t I, Max?”

“You don’t have to kill me.” She tried to stay calm to persuade him, but her voice shook, nonetheless. “We can find a way to work this out.”

“I can’t believe you think I would kill you. I’m not a violent person.” Pete rubbed his head and resumed pacing. “The bullets in this gun aren’t for you, Max. Don’t you get it? The bullets are for Angus.” He raised his head, rampant triumph gleaming from his eyes. “With him gone, we can finally be together. Just you and me.”

Suffocating panic swamped her as she struggled to get air into her lungs. *Please, not Angus.* “You don’t have to do that, Pete. I’ll come with you right now. We can leave this town and start another life somewhere else.”

“It’s too late, Max.” He walked over, picking up a coil of rope he must have left on the table. With his free hand, he shoved her into one of the dining chairs. One hand pressed on her shoulder, the other kept his gun trained at her head. “I chose you, Max. And I was the only one who would dedicate all these years to having you. But you clearly don’t appreciate my patience or the sacrifices I’ve made along the way.”

Her mind scrambled to catch up. “You mean since you came to work for me? Is that what you mean?”

"I knew you wouldn't understand." He reached into the pocket of his dusty jeans and pulled something out, holding it up for her to see. Leaning to peer at it, she realized with a jolt of shock that it was a worn photograph of her at her tenth birthday party. "See? I chose you. You were perfect."

Her stomach lurched as her frazzled mind tried to sort out the implications. "Where did you get that?"

"From your photograph album." His lips peeled back from his teeth in a macabre grin. "Your mother thought it was that deadbeat ex-husband of hers who was coming after her, didn't she? She didn't even consider anyone else, especially not that nice young man who repaired her garage."

She stared at him in horror, her mind racing in a terrifying direction. "Please, Pete, we can work something out. Don't do this." Trying to steady her voice, she searched for any words that might reach him.

Ignoring her, he bound her body, his expression now filled with stony resolve. He'd set the gun down to do it, just far enough that she couldn't reach it without excessive risk. Looping four coils of rope around both her arms and legs limited her options. She expanded her chest and arms a bit to gain some wiggle room. Trying to calm her breathing, she considered her rapidly diminishing options.

Reaching over, he snatched her cellphone off the kitchen counter, shoving it in his jacket pocket. "I'll untie you when it's all over. I just can't afford to let you warn him." The dogs bayed in confusion from the other bedroom as he stalked out the front door, slamming it behind him.

She'd never dreamt it could be Pete causing her problems. Never considered him for a moment. Maybe Alan, before he died, or even Todd Priestly, the arrogant ass, but never Pete, her sweet-tempered worker.

Now she sat alone in the dining room, tied up and helpless, without even the dogs to help her.

With a clarity born of desperation, she suddenly remembered a crime show she'd seen on television where a bound person had smashed the chair they were strapped into against something. She rocked back and forth, feeling some give in the ropes. What would be the hardest thing in her house?

Casting around, she saw the granite countertop. Shuffling over to it in an awkward bucking motion cost her precious minutes, the ropes digging blistering troughs into her skin. She finally made it across the room. Tilting on two chair legs, she gained enough momentum to hit the opposite side of the chair against the stone, rocking over and over. When a few spindles finally gave, taking the top piece with them, she almost toppled to the floor.

Once she managed to wiggle one arm out, she pulled loop after loop of rope off until she broke free. Pete had taken her cellphone and cut her home line. Nate had gone out with Emma. Angus's safety depended on her.

****

The strange sound brought Angus into the living room to investigate its origin. Coming to a stumbling halt, he stared at the gun in Pete's hand with disbelief. The other man stood framed by the cracked open glass patio doors, a twisted look of triumph on his face.

"What are you doing here?"

"Shut up," Pete snarled. "You're not in charge here. I am. You have to do whatever I say."

"Okay." He ignored his speeding pulse. "You're in charge."

"Don't patronize me," he spat. "You chose your destiny."

Because he didn't understand the other man's words, he stayed silent, trying to assess the situation.

"You couldn't stay away from her, could you? You just had to steal everything from me, you greedy bastard."

The pieces started to fall into place then: the motion he'd seen in the woods and the incidents at Max's house. He tried to recall anything he'd read about how to deal with a person bent on violence. "Pete, let's sit down, man to man, and talk about this."

"You're not my boss, big shot. You're not allowed to tell me what to do."

He kept his tone calm. "You're a good man. Tell me what you want, and let's see if we can work it out."

## Chapter Nineteen

Lurching to her feet, Max peered through the front window into the shadowed night. Dread threatened to paralyze her. The dogs howled from their enclosure, sensing danger, but she couldn't worry about them right now.

She needed a weapon. She didn't have any guns, and the only thing she could think of was the cast iron pan Angus had left in her kitchen. Running back to grab it, she made the decision to breach the darkness as quickly as she could, hoping her heart wouldn't just stop beating from the panic. She had no other alternatives, and praying for courage, she flung open the door.

A sliver of a moon helped her fumble her way as she headed for the familiar route. A flashlight would only draw attention to her approach. Running across the lawn, she slipped through the wooden fence, trying to control her gasping breath as she headed toward his kitchen window. A light shone through the glass from that spot. It acted like a beacon, drawing her there. She could try to look in and determine where Pete and Angus were located without being seen.

Her sweating hands forced her to grasp the pan tighter, terrified she would hear a shot before she could reach them. Her breath heaved in and out like an asthmatic. She tried to quiet it as she reached the window, easing up to peek inside.

*Nothing*.

Suddenly, she heard their words coming to her in a muted murmur. First Angus, whose voice filled her with relief.

She heard cursing, and Pete's voice sounded different than it ever had, the words ground out from somewhere deep in his throat. "I deserve to have her. And we can't work that out, can we, because she wants you instead of me. You're responsible for this mess, not me."

She snuck to the living area window and there they were, standing facing each other, with Pete's gun pointed up at Angus's chest. Her target's back faced the sliding doors, and that gave her an idea. She counted on them being unlocked as she made her way to them. Hearing the murmur of Angus's soothing words as well as Pete's resentful response, she prayed for just a few more minutes.

Before she rounded the corner, she pulled her shoes off so their sound on the deck wouldn't alert him. Slipping up the steps in her socked feet, she gripped the pan, knowing she would only have one strong swing to get it right. She saw with relief the doors were apart. Inching the door open enough to enter, she saw a flicker in Angus's eyes as he registered her presence. Pete was waving his free arm in agitation and rambling on in an incoherent babble. She used that distraction to slide inside.

Lifting the pan above shoulder level, she swung hard at Pete's head as Angus dove off to the side. Pete's finger jerked the trigger as the pan hit his head. A gunshot followed the sound of the impact, the loud noises shocking in the normally serene room. Angus lunged, vaulting on top of Pete when he fell and shoving the gun out of reach. "Are you okay?" he shouted, keeping the other man pinned, just in case.

"Y-yes," she answered, the word stuttering out as she held back tears of relief.

"Call Ian. We need him and an ambulance asap."

She could hear Pete groaning as she grabbed Angus's cellphone off the counter and made the call. Within a few torturous minutes, the wail of sirens sounded, the racket enough to wake the neighborhood.

Their captive alternated between swearing and crying, which upset her even more. Angus continued talking to him in a calm tone until Ian ran in through the front door with two deputies.

He pulled up, puffing, next to her. "What the hell is going on here, Max?"

She explained as well she could as the deputies took charge of Pete and let the paramedics look at him. In moments, they trundled him out of the door on a stretcher, his hands cuffed to the sides of the gurney. His curses and threats echoed behind him.

"I'll be damned. He always seemed like one of the good guys," Ian said. "I'm sorry, Max." He grinned, shaking his head. "You hit him with a frying pan?"

"It was the only weapon I could think of."

Angus came to stand beside her, putting an arm around her shoulders. "Hey, don't laugh. It worked."

Nate rushed through the door, his face pale. He slowed when he saw them, heaving in a breath. "You guys took about a year off my life, you know."

"Sorry, Nate." Max reached out to pat his arm.

He wiped sweat from his forehead. “The dogs were howling so loud, we could hear them as we drove by the house. We had just found the ropes, and I freaked out. I was searching for you when I heard the sirens.”

“Where’s Emma?” Max asked.

Hearing her name, she poked her head in the door. “Daddy made me stay outside.”

“It’s okay, now, Em,” Max said. She ran to join them.

She looked up. “Have you got another boo-boo, Agnus?”

“No, Emma. Max took care of me.”

She snuggled against her leg. “That means you get cotton candy and ice cream.”

Max leaned down and hugged her back. “Sounds like a great deal to me.”

Ian told them they could come into the office and give their statements the following day. When he left to follow the ambulance into town, Nate took Emma off to bed. Max and Angus sat, exhausted, the rescued dogs asleep in the corner of the living room.

“I can’t believe you ran through the pitch dark to help me, like an avenging angel. I’m so incredibly proud of you.”

“Don’t be too proud.” She let out a long sigh. “I thought my heart was going to stop, it hammered so hard.”

“But it didn’t.”

She shook her head. “No, but it came close. I could barely breathe. And I seriously thought I might wet myself when I saw his gun aimed at your heart.”

“Close only counts in horseshoes and hand grenades,” he answered.

"Oh, I like that saying. And it's true, I guess." She paused. "I still feel sorry for getting so angry with you."

"It's okay." He smiled. "I get a little pushy sometimes."

"Ya think?" She moved over and sat on his lap. "It's okay. You have other qualities I'm quite fond of."

"I would certainly hope so." He kissed her cheek. "Can I give you something to think about?"

"Maybe. If you make me something to eat. All of a sudden, I'm starving."

He nodded, heading into the kitchen. Pausing, he pointed to the frying pan. "I'm never going to think about that the same way again. I feel like we should engrave your name on it or something."

She watched as he cracked eggs into a bowl, then dragged cheese and tomato from the fridge. When he patted the stool, she went over and sat. "You like this house, right?"

"Of course I like it. The best builder in town created it."

"Well, if you really like it, you might consider that it's the perfect size for two adults and three dogs." He poured the eggs into the pan.

She started to stutter.

He continued on, calmly ignoring her. "I think Nate and Emma are due for an upgrade. Your place would suit them to a tee."

"Nate and Emma like their house," she stammered. "It's where they've always lived."

He shook his head. "He thinks it's getting a little small, now that Emma's growing up. We've discussed it."

"How convenient." When had the two of them become close enough to gang up on her? Nate was pretty picky when it came to making friends. Angus had just crept into all their lives and changed everything.

She could smell the cheesy scent of the omelet as he slid it out of the pan. It made her stomach gurgle. Dividing it into two pieces, he put each one on a separate plate and handed her a fork. Sitting next to her, he gave her a nudge. "Eat up."

It took a few minutes to eat and, finishing, he pushed away from the bar. "You have no more excuses. Tonight, you proved to all of us that you can conquer your fear." He grinned. "You just needed the right motivation, although I'm not sure I'll be thanking Pete anytime soon."

Max savored the last delicious bite, thinking about everything he'd said. He had a point. She just kept getting in her own way. There had never been anyone like him, no one who even came close. He understood her in a way few people did. Maybe terror helped put things in perspective. *Time to take a chance*.

Reaching out, she squeezed his hand. "When should I move in?"

When they woke the next morning, she said, "There's something unbelievable I have to tell you."

"Okay." He sat up, propping himself against the headboard.

She took a deep breath. "I think Pete killed my mother."

He turned to face her, his eyes widening. "What did I miss?"

"Last night, he said something to the effect of that he chose me and Mom had never suspected him.

Apparently, he had repaired our garage. I mean, I remember it being done, but nothing about the people who did it."

"How old were you when she died?"

"Ten."

"That's pretty disturbing." He rubbed her back. "Sorry. It's a lot to take in, all at once. Why didn't you say something last night?"

"I needed some time to process. I wanted to make sure he really said it the way I remembered. Everything happened so fast. When he said that, I realized he really was going to kill you."

"How old is he now?"

She shrugged. "Late forties, I think."

"And your mother's murder was—what—twenty years or so ago?"

"Twenty-five."

"So, he would have been early twenties." He grimaced. "I guess in his sick mind, that wasn't a big age difference between the two of you."

"I have to tell Ian."

"Of course, you do. We need to go to the office and fill out our statements, anyway."

Saying he was surprised to see them so early, Ian waved them to chairs in his cramped office. When she recounted what Pete had said, his immediate response was, "Holey Moley. Are you serious?" Then he told them to sit tight and made some calls. After he finished, he said, "Jeff is freaking out."

At Angus's blank look, he explained. "Jeff was the sheriff when Max's mom died. He's retired now. But he never thought it was Max's dad who made all the threats." He shook his head in disbelief. "He's feeling vindicated, but a little freaked out that it was Pete all this time. I guess he knew his father."

"I ran into Jeff last year. He said it had been his only unsolved murder." Max sighed. "Who was the other call to?"

"The current sheriff over there. He's going to come and talk to us later today." He opened a drawer and pulled out some forms. "Now that you guys are here, let's get the official statements out of the way. Then we'll see if Pete will confirm what he told you. Maybe we can finally close your Mom's case."

****

"You're awfully quiet," Angus said as she slumped on the couch in her house two days later. The previous day, they'd found out Pete had admitted to everything, had, in fact, boasted about it.

She tapped her fingers against the coffee table. "I still can't believe my Mom's murderer was right under my nose for so many years. And that I hired him. You'd think he would have given himself away at some point. It's a lot to take in, I guess."

"Does it help to talk about it?"

"It does help a bit."

"How much do you remember from the night your mother died?"

Sitting up, she straightened her clothes. "All of it, unfortunately. I mean, it doesn't panic me the way it used to, but you never forget. It's like a scene from a movie that plays in your head sometimes."

"Will you tell me about it?" He sat beside her and took her hand. The whole story poured out of her, her frantic escape and hearing the shot that ended her mother's life.

"You were brave, even then." He hugged her. "Your mother came up with the contingency plan. That's impressive on its own merits. But then, you carried it out, even though you must have been terrified. She would have been so proud of you."

"I didn't feel brave," she answered. "The very opposite, in fact."

"Courage isn't the absence of fear. It's acting despite feeling fear."

"I guess that's true." She settled her head against his shoulder. "Can I ask you a favor?"

"Anything."

"I thought I might go visit my mom's grave this afternoon. Will you come with me?"

"I would be honored."

After lunch, they took the winding county road to Macon, just two towns away. She pointed out her old house as they drove by. It looked like any other neighborhood house with no warning of its tragic history of horror.

The serene cemetery had neat rows of gravestones huddled under a spreading canopy of trees. The only sounds were the whispering breeze and an occasional birdcall. She parked toward the back and beckoned him to follow as they exited the truck.

They walked, hand in hand, until they reached a small, gray marker. It had the name, Carolyn Maxwell, and the simple message Rest in Peace along with the relevant dates. Adding up the years, Angus realized she had died at the age of thirty-nine. *Such a waste.*

"Is it going to freak you out if I talk to her? It's just what I do. I find it comforting."

"It won't bother me. Go right ahead."

Sitting cross-legged on the ground, Max told her mother about what had happened and how they had finally discovered the truth about that night. It took a while, and she rested her fingers on the stone as she talked. When she finished, she reached out for help getting to her feet.

With a smile for him, she thought about his earlier words and concluded, “You would have been proud of me, Mom. I didn’t let your murderer win. I only wish you were here to meet Angus.” After a minute of silence, she brushed away a few tears. “Okay, that’s enough for today.”

She hugged him and turned toward the exit. He reached out to her, smiling when she took his hand and squeezed. Linked together by that simple touch, they headed home.

**A word about the author...**

Dianne McCartney has been writing for seventeen years and has won sixty writing awards in contests across Texas and Oklahoma. She is a long-standing member of the Oklahoma Writers Federation, Inc. and the Rose Rock Writers.

http://www.diannemccartney.com
Twitter: @AuthorDMcC
Instagram: diannemccartney1200